# HEATHER GRACE STEWART

# Lauren
## from last night
### A LOVE AGAIN NOVEL

## ILLUSTRATED BY KAYLA MAE STEWART

Lauren From Last Night

By Heather Grace Stewart

Copyright 2020 by Heather Grace Stewart, Graceful Publications
Edited by Jennifer Bogart

Illustrations copyright 2020 by Kayla Mae Stewart

Cover design copyright 2020 by Heather Grace Stewart

Print ISBN: 978-1-988248-05-9
Digital ISBN: 978-1-988248-04-2

For Bill and Kayla, with love and gratitude.

Thanks to my eagle-eyed editor Jennifer Bogart, to my agent Stephanie Hansen and her dedicated team at Metamorphosis Literary Agency, to Dreamscape Media, and to everyone who believed in this book.

Most of all, thanks to the University of Calgary students who inspired this story.

# 1: WE ARE SNOWFLAKES IN MATCHING CROP TOPS

## Lauren's Diary – KEEP OUT!

*Wait a minute. How the bloody hell did you find my diary key? I hid it behind Brittany's white wine in the mini fridge! Well, now that you're here, you can read one, just one diary entry before we get to the really good stuff. I wouldn't want to give away too many spoilers. We all need a few good surprises in life, right?*

*I used to think I was unique. Deep down, we all want to believe that about ourselves, don't we? It's hard enough to roll out of bed and make yourself look a little less Walking Dead-like for school every morning, but once I read that everyone on Earth is made up of ninety-nine point nine percent of the same genetic material? Total letdown.*

### THE DAILY GAZETTE

*(Sadly, my Coventry, England paper also fails to be unique. It's like every failing newspaper in the world)*

Whether you're from Somalia, Santiago or Sudbury, your genetic make-up is strikingly similar to that of every other person on Earth, an analysis concludes today.

The study found that all humans are 99.9 percent identical and, of that tiny 0.1 percent difference, 94 percent is among individuals from the same populations and only six percent between individuals from different populations.

*I read this scientific fact the summer before my first year at the University of Warwick. That was before everything I knew to be real came crashing down; before I felt like I'd spent the first twenty years of my life shoveling a foul-smelling pile of laughing "Fooled Ya!" shite.*

*Last fall, one tiny newspaper article didn't feel too earth-shattering. Still, I cut it out (My name is Lauren, and I have a clipping problem. I clip and save interesting articles faster than an eighty-year-old can say Bingo!) and posted it on my corkboard beside my favorite photo of me and my then-boyfriend, Alex, embracing. Two weeks later, Alex became Lexy, and my parents announced they were divorcing.*

*Maybe that article was more significant in my life than I thought. I thought Lexy's transitioning and Dad moving out of my childhood home were what propelled me to move from England to Edwin Cove, Ontario, Canada for a two-term exchange at Terry Fox University (TFU). I wanted a fresh start for second year.*

*I found this article among a dozen small Polaroids in the box I still have to unpack, and now I realize it was way more than that. I wanted to make a mark. I wanted to stand out from all* the other heartbroken girls at school. I wanted to prove I was as special as a sparkling snowflake, just like Dad told me when I was in preschool. I remember he said that while handing me my red left-handed scissors with his left hand so that I could make a Christmas mobile for Mum. I also recall thinking that my mobile looked like everyone else's in the class, and even at that young age, I wondered why parents enunciated the words "special" and "gifted" but always said "challenged" and "unique" in hushed tones. Dad hasn't bothered to spend time with me in six months. And yet, he was none too pleased to hear I was taking second year in Canada. I'm sure he'll be ringing any day, wondering how I ended up sparkling in my not-so-special American Eagle crop top beside 245 other girls named Lauren.

How do I even begin to explain how my love life (or lack thereof) came to be broadcast across the Internet, TV and YouTube?

How did my life become a headline story the whole bloody world is laughing about?

Heather Grace Stewart

# 2: NIETZSCHE WAS A NUTBAR

## LAUREN

### One week earlier

"Friedrich Nietzsche. Fascinating stuff."

"Oh God, no. This is depressing," I say, still looking down. "I want to hang myself!" I slam *Beyond Good and Evil* shut.

I'm honestly relieved someone is giving me an excuse to stop reading my assigned book. More like Beyond Boring. By page eighteen, I wanted to stab my eyeballs with a fork.

But now, things are looking up. Way up. The someone standing before me is a tall hottie in blue jeans, a fitted black t-shirt and a tan suede jacket. His skin is a beautiful shade of golden brown, and he has a muscular build, wavy chocolate-brown hair and striking hazel eyes. As he smiles at me and absent-mindedly scratches the stubble on his chin, I realize he reminds me of a Spanish Shawn Mendes. That singer is delicious, but this guy is simply yummy. He's the whipped cream on a Shawn Mendes sundae.

"Please, don't hang your lovely self. That would be such a tragedy. At least let me get to know you first." He smirks. "Can I join you?" The light Spanish lilt to his words is the most melodic song I've heard in days. My mind says no, but his sexy closed-lip smile makes me want to stand up and shout yes, yes, *yes*!

I glance over my shoulder. She said we'd only be here five minutes, but my roommate Brittany is still chirpsing the bartender. I'm not surprised; she actually friended our bus driver the other day. Our bus driver! How does she do it?

I try to be outgoing. I try to meet new people. I even let Brittany drag me to this off-campus basement bar with its sticky floors, wood-panel walls and twangy old country tunes set to shuffle. I can be social. It's just that I'd much rather be back at the dorm in my pajamas binge-watching Netflix.

"Well, I'm here with a friend," I say, nervously twirling my long brown side-braid. "She told me she'd walk me to the library, but obviously, she's got other plans..." I nod my head in Brittany's direction. Did I just admit to a gorgeous boy that I'm going to the library on the first Friday night of the school year? Lex will have beef with me about this.

"No worries, I just wanted to talk. I wasn't even going to buy you a drink or anything."

"You weren't? That's cheap of you." I smile up at him, proud of my newfound sassiness. The beer I just finished must be going straight to my head.

"Uh, no, I mean, if you want one, or water... I could get drinks for you and your friend... if you're of age that is..." He shoves both his hands in his pockets, seeming unsure what to do next.

I motion for him to take a seat at my table, and he pulls out the chair, turns it, and sits so he's leaning against the wooden back. Then he hangs a small, wooden handled umbrella over the top of the chair. Hmm. He's unusual. I like unusual. Suddenly feeling self-conscious, I flatten out a crease in my light blue off-the-shoulder blouse. I regret not bothering to change when Brittany dragged me out here. There's quite possibly a chocolate pudding stain on my left boob, but I'm not about to look down there now, not while he's staring so intently at me.

"I'm twenty-one. You're thinking I look young for my age, right?"

"You look about nineteen. But that'll be good news someday," he answers.

"I have been told I look young, but I never did the fake ID thing. I could legally drink at eighteen in England—that's where I'm from—but I never liked the taste of beer until this year."

"Me too. My father's rancid home brews gave me a bad first impression. I thought all beer tasted like feet." His expression, nose and lips scrunched up like a ninety-year-old man, makes me laugh.

"I'm Lauren," I say and hold out my hand. I almost say "Green" at the end there, but then Mum screams at me in my mind, "Stranger Danger!" and I swallow the word, so it comes out sounding more like Lauren-gah. Bloody fracking hell. He must think I'm on a bender.

"Hi." He takes my hand in his, and I feel a surge of electricity traveling from our fingers all the way up my arm, across my neck and breasts. I take my hand away faster than I want to.

"I'm Samuel Sanchez; Sam for short. I was supposed to meet someone here, but it looks like she stood me up." He glances at his phone and pouts, and my heart skips a beat. Those full lips!

"Oh no, that's not nice. Did you know her long?"

"Last week. Tinder. Looks like swiping right was my worst idea this semester."

"I hate to break it to you, but the semester's only been a week so far," I say.

He laughs and relaxes his arms over the back of the chair.

"Then things can only improve from here," he says. "So, do you like it here so far? I was born in Cuba, but we left when I was four, and I haven't been back in years. I haven't been outside of Canada in a decade. My parents moved here from Toronto, feeling that Edwin Cove was a smaller, safer town. They're too afraid to travel anymore."

"Really? I've been lucky to have seen a lot of the world over the years because my parents took me traveling with them in the Doctors without Borders program... this was all before... before my dad left..." I let my voice trail off and try to think of something more positive to say. "I think Canada is the prettiest nation in the world. I still marvel at how its lakes sparkle."

"Have you seen Sandbanks yet?" I like that he's observant enough to avoid any further questions about my father. He leans in towards me as he speaks, and I catch a whiff of his aftershave, or maybe it's his bodywash. It's understated: a spicy, modern scent that isn't overpowering.

"Sadly, no, I've only been here thirteen days." I look at Sam more closely. It's a shame no one's invented a BS Detector app yet. He seems sweet. Trustworthy. But I shouldn't reveal too much to someone I've just met in a bar.

"Woah! You're new here. I had no idea. Let me buy you a drink. Please. I'm driving, but I'll get you something." He gets up and starts for the bar, calling over his shoulder. "A welcome drink from a student who's roamed the TFU halls for far too long." He chuckles. "What'll it be?"

"Oh, well, if they don't serve it warm like back home, I'll just try a pint of anything," I call back, loud enough for Brittany to take notice. She glances over at me and mouths, "You okay?" She clearly wants my answer to be yes, so despite that she's looking drunk as a skunk, I give her a little nod. She's parked on the bar stool in front of a colossal-sized martini like it's her regular spot, pulling down her crop top and tiny black leather skirt every three seconds as she watches the bartender pour my beer and a cola for Sam. I think there's a little bit of drool in the left corner of her mouth.

I get up, slap a five-dollar bill on the bar, grab the beer and raise it in a 'cheers.'

"It was a nice thought, but I can take care of myself," I say. I like him, and I know he meant well, but I prefer human decency over chivalry. I'd like to think a woman could open a door for a man who's got his hands full and he'd think nothing of it. I still see men looking at me sideways when I do so.

The music has changed, and I look behind Sam's shoulder to see why. Two guitarists and a drummer are on the small, poorly lit stage at the front the room, singing a cover I recognize as a ballad by Dan and Shay. I don't know country music as well as British pop, but I've heard this band because Brittany played them non-stop last week, and we share a room at Viola Desmond (Desie) Hall. I am so going to regret not paying more for a single room.

There are only four occupied tables tonight, and it doesn't look like anyone's getting up to line dance anytime soon, but this live music definitely beats the shite they were playing before.

Sam is holding his drink, not moving. He's just looking at me. "Have I made you uncomfortable?" he asks, shouting above the band.

"No. I just like to take care of myself, that's all." I raise my voice as well. I wasn't planning on dating anyone this year, not after July. In July, Alex... I mean Lexy... took my beating heart from my hands and puréed it into a tomato paste. She didn't mean to, of course, and she's in more pain than I am or ever will be. I can't deny how much it hurts, though. How I still wonder if I was part of the problem. I know I'm not supposed to call it a problem. Buggernuts. Why is love so complicated? Why can't it ever be easy?

And yet, for some reason, I want to know more about this guy. He intrigues me. Besides, the band is good, and Brittany isn't leaving any time soon. "Sit with me. I want to hear why Nietzsche doesn't put you to sleep."

Sam laughs, takes a sip of his cola and sits back down, his chair facing backwards again. "It was a line, and a rotten one at that. I like some of his philosophies, but honestly, I just wanted to meet the girl reading Nietzsche in a country bar." His eyes crinkle at the corners, and I feel my cheeks grow hot.

"You've studied him too?" It's stuffy in this small room, but the beer is cold and refreshing, so I take a long swig. The band is playing a livelier tune, so we lean in a little closer. Sam has switched his chair around, so we're sitting side by side, facing the band. I lean my left ear in a little so I can hear him better. When he answers, his lips accidentally brush against my cheek, and I feel the hairs on my arms stand up.

"I studied him a little, first year, but I had a change of heart that year." He inhales and looks at his lap, as though he's deciding if he should say something else, something more personal, but he only adds, "I'm in my third year of med school now. I'm clerking in emergency medicine."

"Oh, that's cool. I can't take med school courses here. I'm limited in the courses I can take as an exchange student, so I'm just enjoying my second year. Taking philosophy and even some Spanish." He smiles at that. I hesitate a second, then add, "I'm here trying to live outside of my comfort zone."

"Here in Canada, or here in this bar?"

"Both." I chuckle. "I'm not much of a bar person."

"I kind of noticed that, since there were people dancing on the speakers over there an hour ago while you had your nose in Nietzsche." He smiles.

"There were? How did I miss that?" Sometimes I get so absorbed in what I'm doing.

"Ah, see, Nietzsche had you mystified."

"More like borderline suicidal," I groan. The worst part is I have to read this book outside of class, but we already discussed 200 pages from *Untimely Meditations*.

"Don't joke about suicide or religion, politics or gender equality." I can tell by his tone that he's far from serious about this. "We're studying at a major university. We're supposed to be respectable, proper, educated folks. None of those things can be funny."

"Respectable? You're kidding, right? I guess you didn't see the girls in my common room tonight, flat on their backs and half-naked, funneling beer?"

Sam winces. "Ah, beer bong: where classy girls stumble out wearing their own vomit. It's wild over there, huh? And you're not into that kind of thing?"

"I'm fun," I say, hearing the defensiveness in my voice. "I mean, I can be. I just don't like losing control of my inhibitions like that. It was so loud at the dorm, I said I wanted to go to the library, then Brittany said she'd walk me, but she brought me here first..." There I go again, sounding like a fun sponge who's only interested in studying.

"So, I won't be expecting you up there dancing with the band tonight," he says as he leans in close.

"Never say never," I say in his ear, once again surprising myself.

Heather Grace Stewart

## 3: DEAD PHILOSOPHERS CAN BLOW ME

### SAM

I am going to marry this girl.

I know. I know what you're thinking. I sound like some cheesy Hollywood actor in a classic romance film, maybe a black and white one starring Bing Crosby. Is he the one who danced on the ceiling? Never mind, you know what I mean to say.

I, Sam Sanchez, am a hopeless romantic. Always have been, always will be. But there's nothing romantic about this. I'm being practical about my feelings and basing them on what I know about Lauren from the last few hours of chatting with her. The situation, however? That's very likely hopeless. Bring me my swim shorts and a life preserver; I'm about to dive into a sea of hopelessness.

Lauren is beautiful, she's smart, she's independent, and she's funny. She's totally out of my league, yet she's still sitting here with me. This is my lucky night. Knowing me, I'll probably blow it in a big fat Fail kind of way. *¡Me resbala!* I don't care. I have to get her number. You don't meet a woman like Lauren every day.

The band is on a break, so this is the perfect opportunity to speak with her without having to shout above the noise. Lauren's already turning her chair back around to face the table, and I follow suit. Pleased to find her staying, I grab my black backpack off the floor beside my feet, set it on the third chair, and ask her if she'd like another beer.

"God, no thanks, this is my second. I'll be on the floor if I'm not careful."

"Like your friend?" I motion with my head over to the girl at the bar who's still flirting with the bartender. Lauren rolls her eyes and sighs.

"Technically, Brittany's not my mate. Forced-mate. We're roommates. I thought this was a library, remember? She tricked me."

I can't help laughing at that one. "What gave it away first? The plastic jugs of beer on every table instead of books? The pool table where there should be a librarian in the corner?"

"I knew, of course, that it wasn't a library when we were outside." She chuckles. "I begrudgingly entered the bar, hoping she wouldn't be this long talking with Jason."

Begrudgingly. I adore how she uses words. She's obviously well-read. I'm mesmerized by her mouth, how it moves as she speaks—those thick pink lips. I have to adjust my jeans without her looking. Everything she does is a turn-on.

Lauren must assume by my silence that I'm offended, because she adds, "Of course, there's been a silver lining, meeting you, but I really did want to study Nietzsche tonight."

I shake my head, grazing a finger and thumb across my stubble beard as I try to formulate my thoughts. "Thanks, but I'm confused. I thought I saved you from a near-death experience."

"Yes!" She swallows her last sip of beer and slams the glass on the table. I almost expect it to shatter. "He's an enormous bore, but I still have to read this whole book for Monday. Why do we have to listen to long-ago dead people wax philosophical? Why?"

She's cute when she gets riled up. "Because they enlighten us about how to live," I say.

"How to live? How to live? He's dead! Dead guys don't get to have an opinion on how to live!" She's slurring every second word now. I bite my lower lip, so I don't laugh.

"Plus, I'll have you know, Sam Sanchez," I lose my breath a little as she draws out the 'm' in my name, "I have beef with almost everything Nietzsche says about individualized greatness. He says that to become great, we must overcome the self and set oneself apart from the human masses."

"What's so wrong about that?" I lean in closer. "Individuality is a great thing in my opinion."

"Well, for one, Nietzsche didn't have the Internet. Everyone is attempting greatness on the Internet, and they're fucking failing at it."

"That's bare jokes," I laugh, trying to impress her with my limited knowledge of British slang.

"Right?" She cocks her head to the side a little. "Hey. You speak British." She leans forward, smiling at me with her eyes.

"Very little. I know you eat bangers and mash."

"Hell no! That stuff is rubbish senior citizens eat. Well, my sister Natalie likes it, but she's already married with kids, and that's old in my opinion."

I'm delighted to discover this nasty side of sweet little Lauren. It's entertaining.

"My go-to comfort food is pizza. Thick crust. None of that thin-crusted shite. Thick-crusted pizza's totally bangin'." She twirls the end hairs on her long braid with two fingers and looks at me for a second as she finishes her sentence. Then something flashes across her eyes. It's as if she's just remembered I'm not family. Studying her in this moment of recognition, I think she's going to clam up, but to my surprise, she keeps on speaking.

"All I'm saying is, if we've been so enlightened by all these dead philosophers, we've done a bloody awful job of using their knowledge to improve the peace or the welfare of this planet."

I start to nod my head in amusement and agreement, but as Lauren says the word "improve" there's a loud popping sound near the bar. It sounds like an enormous champagne bottle has exploded behind us. Wait... now it sounds like a crew of firemen have dragged a hose into the bar, and they're deliberately spraying our table.

"Blow me, Mother Trucker!" Lauren shouts in surprise, her face scrunched in disgust as she leaps from her chair. It falls to the floor with a loud crash. She's drenched in beer foam: a wet cat left out in the storm, shaking her fur and whiskers. I almost imagine her hiding under the table right now, licking her paws, trying to regain her dignity. I cough to disguise that I'm laughing at her adorableness and remind myself to read the entire Urban dictionary—UK edition—when I get home.

I feel wet foam splattering my head too, but no amount of lip biting or coughing can disguise my laughter now. I stand up, grab Lauren's book off the table, and throw it into my backpack. She stands as still as a statue and just stares at me, eyes wide. Half a second later, she throws her arms up in the beer-filled air, twirling in circles as she joins me in belly laughter. People are screeching and running for cover to no avail—unless they sprint for the door—but it seems they can't. The floor is covered in slippery foam, and the culprit, a shiny gold beer tank that's burst open, is spraying everyone up to two meters away.

"What a waste of perfectly good beer!" I shout as I watch people wiping their faces with their shirts.

Jason the bartender, has valiantly rushed over to the tank to try to stem the flow with a plastic bin, but his efforts are hopeless. He's getting absolutely drenched. Brittany is still sitting on her bar stool, soaked to the skin and laughing at Jason.

"Friday night foam party! We planned it, honest!" Jason yells to everyone, waving his arms madly at a group of students skating in the foam. A few of them seem to be heading for the front door. "Come back! Lick it off the floor, and it's free!" He laughs.

The gold tank is gushing beer at an alarming rate. Lauren and I are standing in a light beer shower, gaping at the scene, until I remember my blue umbrella. I grab it from the chair where it's hanging and open it over Lauren first. She looks at me, gives me the sweetest smile, and moves in closer, so we're sharing the umbrella.

So. This is how I'm spending my first Friday night, third year of TFU Meds.

Under a blue umbrella, in a beer shower with a beautiful girl.

"Are you sure you can carry her up the steps yourself?"

"Yeah, I've got this."

I look over at Lauren in the passenger seat beside me, then at Brittany, semi-conscious in the backseat of my old pickup truck. She's flat on her back, mumbling nonsense. There's a long string of drool coming out of the left side of her mouth, and one of her legs is hanging out the open window.

"Justin is my baby. He's all mine, and she can't have him or his baby because he's my baby..." she's mumbling as she smacks her lips together.

"Is she okay?" Not waiting for Lauren to answer, I unbuckle my seatbelt and rush around the truck, gently placing her foot back inside as I open the back door. I parked right in front of Viola Desmond Hall and know I need to hurry before a cop dings me for being in a no-stopping zone.

"I've got this, I've got this," Lauren says firmly, trying to lift Brittany's head and pull her out the other side. I'm getting quite a show here, since she's wearing a miniskirt, and apparently is just like that famous Brittany who doesn't believe in underwear. It's far from classy and besides that, Brittany's legs, hair... everything about her reeks of micro-brewery.

I'm sure I smell like a micro-brewery, too, I've just become accustomed to the smell. The staff at the bar gave Lauren a TFU rugby shirt from the Lost and Found because her blouse and jeans were completely drenched. Now she's wearing only that, like a shirtdress that falls mid-thigh, and black ankle boots. I may as well have been drinking because just looking at her in that outfit makes me feel light-headed.

"I'm a Belieber!" Brittany screeches, kicking one leg so high she almost belts me in the face. Lauren rolls her eyes and sighs.

"Buggernuts, Sam, I don't got this. Can you pull her by the legs, and I'll try to push her out from this end?"

"Come to this side, here." I grunt as I try to pull Brittany out of the truck. "Help me grab her... uh... bottom half once it's out." I think Brittany just passed out, which will make it easier to carry her up those concrete steps.

With Lauren holding her calves, and me supporting her back and head, we manage to lift her up about twenty steps to the landing at the front doors, but now her breathing sounds funny. I hope she doesn't have alcohol poisoning. Maybe I should call...

"Rawwwwwwwlf."

Okay then. Don't have to worry about the alcohol poisoning. When she throws up, it catches us both by surprise, and we end up dropping her on the cement. She doesn't even complain. She just curls up in a ball like she's set to take a nap. I take a step back. *Es una porquería.* Now it reeks like beer and a pig sty around here.

"You know what? She's a handful, and you're a great friend," I say.

"Roomie," she corrects me. "Uh, Sam! Your shoes!" Lauren sounds concerned, and yet, she's laughing whole-heartedly as I perform an awkward side-step dance in the puke. Her cheeks are bright red and she's covering her mouth so I can't see it, but she's definitely laughing.

"It's okay, these were old shoes anyways," I say, moving my upper lip under my nose to try to shield it from the putrid smell below.

"Here!" She opens her army green backpack full of wet clothes and pulls out a small white towel. "My gym towel. You can wipe your shoes with that."

"Thanks." I get as much of the puke off as I can, then see a garbage can by the front door and walk over to toss the towel inside. When I return, Lauren has lifted Brittany to her feet and has her firmly by the waist. She's even got the front glass door propped open with her black boot.

"You've got this." I grin.

"I've got this now, thanks to you." She smiles back.

"So, beer showers, barf showers, fun times, right?"

"It was memorable."

"Can I have your number? I'd love to hang out somewhere... less messy... next time."

"We could try... I just... I'm not much of a texter... and..." She looks down at her foot, then peers inside the doors. I had the same thought: Campus Security. "I think there's an alarm about to sound any second."

"Real quick," I say. "And we can actually talk. Like old people."

Lauren's hands are full, so I pull out my own phone and open my contacts.

"I'd like that. Okay. I think it's five four eight... four zero zero two."

"Five four eight four zero zero two. Got it. Thanks Lauren, it was nice to meet you. I really hope Brittany's feeling okay by morning."

"Me too. I can't wait to get back to my reading..." She gives me the slightest wink, but it's enough to keep me going for days. Then, before I can say buggernuts, she's behind the glass door and the building security officer is helping her hoist Brittany up a small flight of stairs, out of my sight.

I've never felt like this **before**. I saunter down the steps as if walking on a cloud, certain I'm not going to sleep tonight. I'm going to run through everything Lauren said and did in my mind, like a movie. Maybe two or three times. Wondering if I said the right things. Knowing it played out how it was meant to. Knowing this is it: *Amor a primera vista*. Love at first sight.

Heather Grace Stewart

## 4: THEN GOLDILOCKS SAID,
## WHO'S BEEN SHAGGING IN MY BED?

## LAUREN

A phone rings, and I'm abruptly pulled out of a dream. I don't care that it's a "pretty, peaceful" Sencha ring as Brittany puts it, the bloody Mormon Tabernacle Choir could wake me with Amazing Grace, and it wouldn't be peaceful enough. This is Saturday, and Saturdays are made for sleeping in. Now I don't remember what I was dreaming. Something about me jumping on a trampoline, holding hands with all the members of the boy band BTS. Then our trampoline turned into a giant cinnamon roll. I suppose I'm hungry or something.

I slowly roll over, imagining Mum stroking my hair to wake me, the smell of cooked bacon wafting up the stairs. What I'm faced with is more like a nightmare.

"It's Jason, checking up on us! Isn't that sweet?" Brittany giggles as she covers the phone. She thinks she's whispering this to me, but she's fucking loud. She's already dressed—if you can call that mingin' low cut tank top and threadbare leggings dressed—sitting crossed-legged on the twin bed opposite mine, far too chipper for someone who spilled her whole guts on my new friend last night.

"Ugh, go away. I'm cream crackered!" I groan.

"You say the strangest things," Brittany whines, but I'm too knackered to explain.

Lying on my back, I cover my face with my pillow. I can't see if Brittany's offended or not, but then I hear the door slam. At least I'm alone now.

I loved waking up on Saturday mornings when Mum and Dad were still together. Mum would usually come tussle my hair while I was sleeping, gently saying, "Come on love, breakfast," and then if I still wouldn't budge, she'd call Dad. He'd come join us and start tickling me until I had to put a pillow over my head and pull up all the blankets. Mum would find it funny until she didn't, telling him to stop—always the protective mama bear.

"Wake up, you have to go to work, earn your keep," he'd joke. Natalie would saunter in all sleepy-eyed, asking us to stop making so much noise. There'd be a pot of coffee brewing downstairs, and the tantalizing aroma of bacon sizzling on the stove would waft up our old wooden stairs, right to my bed. We had it really good until Dad met Denise. Beautiful, French, twenty years younger than Mum—which could make her my sibling, I know, gross—insistent on getting whatever she wants with no regard for the sanctity of family. I refuse to say her name out loud. She's like Voldemort, but viler.

Dad said he'd made a mistake, but he moved in with that mistake a month after telling us about her. He told me in an email that he'd never been happy with Mum. Never? So, our whole life was a total lie and fabrication? I wrote him back that I thought he was having a midlife crisis or suffering from lack of oxygen to the brain or both. We haven't exchanged words or emails since Easter when he tried to call, and I refused to pick up.

Natalie is more forgiving than I am. She's having weekly brunches with Dad and Denise but hasn't told Mum yet. I'm not sure why she's trying to forge any kind of relationship with that woman, except Denise works in fashion, and my sister wants to be a designer once she goes back to work. She says I should try to see the situation more from Dad's perspective. That marriage is work, and maybe he didn't want to have to work at it so hard. I don't think he's seeing the situation from my perspective or Mum's or Natalie's. I think he's simply serving his own needs.

My older brother, Hank, is a livid as I am, but it's much easier for him to stay out of this mess because he's working for some famous ornithologist on a lovely island off of southern France. He's the one who encouraged me to study in Canada this year. Ever since Mum and Dad divorced, he's been telling me I need to "leap out of the nest without wings on and figure out how to grow them on the way down." I would never jump out of a perfectly good plane without a plan, but I admire his sense of adventure and that he said his home is always open for me. I'm hoping to visit him and his new wife Béa at Spring break, if I can keep my savings account intact. I have just enough for the flight to Cannes, and they said they'd take care of my stay and meals.

I sit up, pull on my warm red slippers, gather my hair into a high ponytail, then check the time on my phone. Eight thirty-six! I will never experience the luxury of sleeping in again, as long as I'm living with Boozey Britt.

As soon as I think of her, she's here again, slamming the door behind her, whining about how Jason is 'playing her,' and she's just found out he's engaged.

I've got it! I know exactly who she sounds like. Moaning Myrtle. Buggernuts, my life's a never-ending *Harry Potter* book.

"I was just talking with Ashley in the common room, and she says you should probably change your sheets." She saunters over to our mini-fridge and pulls out a container of Greek yogurt, then flops down on her bed, her back against the brick wall, and begins eating straight out of the container. This was supposed to be our shared food. I guess she thinks "sharing" is putting her spit into everything I'm also planning to eat.

"What do you mean, change my sheets?" I look down at them.

"Oh, she says she has her high school friend Cassidy visiting, and Cass met Art on our floor, and they kind of hooked up on your bed last night?"

"Art? Do I know this Art?"

"Know? I don't think you do... but like, they were in here." She shrugs her shoulders and then digs her spoon deeper into the bottom of the yogurt container. I try to remember to inhale, but I'm having problems breathing, processing this, and restraining myself from tossing my smart phone at her stupid head.

"But… who let them in?"

"Oh, well me, I guess. I mean I wasn't here, but I told Ashley during the party? That anyone could use our room, you know?"

I stand up and glare at her. "No, I don't know. *It's my bloody room, too, you daft cow!*" I can feel my eyeballs bulging out of their sockets. I take a step back, so I won't take a swing at her. She stares back at me, her pouty mouth wobbling as though holding back tears, like I'm the unreasonable one.

"I'm not drunk." She slams the yogurt on her bedside table and stands. "And if you don't want to be gracious and let people who are visiting this institution use your bed, all you had to do was tell me."

"I didn't think I had to tell you not to let strangers shag in my bed!"

"Maybe it's a British thing. Canadians are nice about stuff like that," she huffs, walks to the door and opens it swiftly, glaring at me one more time.

"Canadians do it in canoes! With mosquitoes biting their butts! They're crunchy granola nutbars!" I shout behind her as she slams the door again. I turn and sit on Brittany's bed, feeling completely violated and disgusted, and my tablet starts ringing. I reach over and instinctively answer the Skype call, not thinking about how enraged I look in this moment. Lex always calls me first thing on weekends.

"Hey, Wren…" she says. I usually don't slip up anymore, calling her "he" by accident, but she never gave up her pet name for me. After all we've been through, I don't mind.

Lex brushes her shoulder length blonde hair off her forehead and pulls it into a blue scrunchie so I can see her face better. When she notices my reddened face, her eyes grow wide.

"Um. What the actual fuck?"

"I'm livid with my roommate. She's a total cow."

"You look like you're about to kill someone."

"Could happen. You wouldn't blame me. She let people shag in my bed!"

"Ew!" Lex makes a funny face, sticking out her tongue, and I feel my blood pressure lowering again. As sad as I've been this past year that I lost the sexy thing we had going on, she's still my best friend forever. It took months of tears and even some screaming and cutting each other off on phone calls, but somehow, we've managed to salvage the friendship. I probably wouldn't have survived my parents' divorce without her. I fell into such a depression, she had to come over every night for a week. As we talked things through, I'd look at her and just forget she used to have short blonde hair and facial hair, that we used to snog. I cried a lot when I lost Alex, but Lex still makes me laugh about bloody stupid things, still knows how to calm me down when I'm having a panic attack.

In the end, when they go to cremate us or put us in the ground, they're all just body parts, right? It's the soul of the person that I'm interested in, and as far as I'm concerned, souls are unisex. Gender fluid, actually, or possibly gender neutral? My mind boggles at the hundreds upon thousands of new terms, and you should have heard Mum going on about it all. I told her that Lexy is my friend and always will be; it doesn't matter how she pees. Although, speaking of that...

"So, did you see that doctor?" As soon as I say it, her expression turns serious.

"Yup. Hormone therapy starts next week."

"Seriously? That fast! You'll be turning a right bitch!" I can't hide my surprise. I'm worried this will change her personality. As if reading my mind, she shakes her head at me.

"Allow that!" She laughs, always way cooler than I ever was with the street slang. I know she means "cut it out," "stop it," but being the bookworm, I'm fixated on how grammatically wrong and confusing it is.

"You're the bitch, babe. Always will be."

"Aw love you too, Lex," I say. "My fam." I bite my lower lip and make a face, realizing I simply can't pull off the slang like her.

"Nice try, Wren. Keep trying," she says, but she sounds unconvinced I'll ever get it right. "Hey, let me show you my new maroon eye liner!" I smile for the first time today as she unzips her new, overflowing makeup bag. I feel so happy for her and decide now's not the time to tell her I met someone last night. Besides, he probably won't even call. He seems different from other guys... more mature... but... I glance at my phone when Lex isn't looking. Nope. Not even a text.

How did I think Sam would be different? Why did I even want him to be? My heart's been through the ringer enough this year. I should be giving it a break.

Lex has just applied her new maroon eyeliner and is staring into the camera, looking damn proud of herself. I know I have to say something, anything but this awkward silence, but...

"What? Tell me," she says.

"It's not that it's my old boyfriend wearing eyeliner! I swear, that's not the problem here!" I chuckle.

"Tell me, Wren," she insists.

"The problem is, it's mingin'! It's like, Rollerskating Rink, 1982!"

She starts to pout, but in seconds she's laughing along with me. I sprawl out on Brittany's bed, tablet held close to my face. Suddenly, I don't feel so lonely or angry anymore. I feel hopeful.

But I'm applying for a single room, A.S.A.P.

## 5: GLASS SLIPPERS SHATTER.

**SAM**

I wake to the delightful memory of strong, independent Lauren hoisting her drunken roommate up the stairs, and the aroma of bacon and eggs. As much as I want to hold onto that image of Lauren, I can't help being distracted by the scent. It's wafting down the stairs into my basement bedroom, seducing me in small circles.

I sit upright in bed. I swear Ma's cooking has magical powers. Usually it takes Pa splashing water on me to wake me up on a day off from clerking.

Grabbing my hospital green drawstring scrubs from the floor beside the bed, I pull them on over my boxers. I dress like this for both work and sleep, so if I'm running late, I don't even have to change. As I get up from the bed and reach for my phone to text Lauren, someone abruptly enters the room.

"Good morning *cariño*!" Ma is holding a laundry basket full of clean clothes.

"Ma! I'm a grown man. You still don't know how to knock?" I pull on my scrub top, then kiss her on the cheek. I'm used to her intrusions in my room and in my life, but I still attempt to stand my ground with her, which is no easy feat. I won an argument with this woman once, and it was harder than getting into Med school.

"I haven't seen you in days, and you raise your voice to me?"

"Ma. It wasn't disrespect, if anything you... oh never mind."

"Never mind? I made you a Canadian breakfast, maybe I will say never mind too." There's a hint of a smile on her lips. She throws the two sweatshirts in her hands at my face. I catch them and place them on the bed.

31

"I can do my own laundry, but thank you, for this time." I put my arm around her shoulder and lead her out of the room and up the basement stairs. She's half my size, but I'm always going to be intimidated by her. She's tough as nails, and she almost always gets her way.

"You will come up for our meal tonight, Samuel?" she turns to ask me as we reach the top of the stairs.

"Ma!" I chuckle as I sit down opposite Pa at our rectangular pine dining table. He looks up from his paper, nods, and takes a slow sip of his Cuban coffee. It smells stronger than usual. I know Ma made the Canadian-style breakfast for me, because usually we just have Cuban crackers with butter in the morning. "I just woke up. I'm just starting breakfast. Can we book one meal at a time?"

"Your mother just wants to know how much to cook is all," Pa says as he pours me some *café con leche* from the silver pot beside him. "I invited our landlord over, so we can discuss building safety some more."

I nod, having already heard him rant about our flimsy back door lock earlier this week and wonder why he never lets my mother read the paper. His English improved drastically when he began working at the bank in Toronto and got even better when he was transferred to the branch here. Ma has been in this country twenty years, but she's still resistant to learning the language. She speaks English only to me, because she knows it's my preference, but she and Pa speak Spanish most of the time.

Unlike Pa, she never wanted to come to Canada. She still thinks everything would be different if we'd never left. Maybe it would be. Maybe our family would be whole again. I do know I wouldn't be training to become a doctor at Edwin Cove General Hospital, and that's everything to me.

I look down at my plate, which Ma has magically filled with roasted potatoes, eggs, bacon, and some Cuban crackers and smile to myself. My parents are being pushy, but it's because they want me here, that's all. I've been spending less and less time at home since my classes started, and my shifts at ECGH have increased.

"It's delicious," I tell Ma, who's still not sitting. She's peeling potatoes at the kitchen counter. I wish she'd just sit with us for once. She hasn't enjoyed breakfast with Pa and I once in this house. She won't say it, but I know it's because she doesn't want to remember what it was like when there were four of us sitting at this table.

"I have to clerk on Sunday. Ten-hour shift," I say.

"You still sure?" Pa pulls his glasses off the bridge of his nose and starts to rub his eyes.

"Sure I want to be a doctor? You know the answer."

"I still think it was a mistake. These loans! You will be paying them off all your life."

"If that's what it takes, Pa, then that's what it takes."

"You couldn't..." Ma has stopped peeling the potatoes and looks at me. She's on the verge of tears. "No one could have done anything," she manages, exhales deeply, and returns to the peeling.

We've had the conversation before, and I'm not in the mood for it again this morning. Staring at my empty plate, I finish my last mouthful of coffee, stand and nod at my parents. "Thanks again. I have studying to get to."

"But tonight? You'll eat with us?" Ma shouts behind me.

"I have plans. I'm sorry."

I leave the kitchen and head downstairs quickly before either of my parents notices the tears on my cheek.

Once inside my room, I close the door, turn on the light, and sit on my bed, head in hands. I can hardly face them. Five years next week. It's been five whole years since my little sister died, but I still blame myself for taking her out that night—for not noticing the van before it was too late, for not having the medical knowledge to save her. I can still see his crazy-ass-eyes behind the wheel as the van slammed into her body. She was sitting on a terrace with bright red tables and chairs, enjoying one of our first mild spring evenings. I was walking back to the table with our coffees, and by the time I got to her lying lifeless on the curb at Yonge, she was bleeding profusely. I picked her limp head up, her hair matted in blood. My eyes scanned the area for someone who could help, but everyone was scattering from the sidewalk, running from harm's way.

"Sierra, stay with us. Stay with me."

"He didn't mean it. Don't. Don't." She was looking right at me, but I could tell she was having problems keeping her eyes open.

"What... don't what..." I could barely get my words out amid my sobs.

"Don't live with... hate... in heart..."

Those were Sierra's last words. Even when she was dying, even though she was murdered by a black-hearted terrorist, my little sister still held onto the hope that our world could one day be a better place.

There's an old photo in a gold frame on my bedside table. Sierra's fourteenth birthday. I pick it up to study it once more. We're standing together on the edge of the CN tower, both of us wearing yellow harnesses and crimson red jumpsuits. She's got her arms wide open and a grin on her face that says she can conquer the world. EdgeWalk. We skipped school and spent the morning of her fourteenth birthday circling the edge of the CN tower, 1,168 feet above the ground. It was one of the most exhilarating moments of my life.

Before she was killed, I used to live for adventure. You'd think it was one of my dumbass schemes, but no, she was the one who convinced me to do it! I remember what she said when she handed me the pamphlet: "We're all dying a little every day, Sam, but are any of us really living?" She was so brave, so full of life, and it was fucking stolen from her.

Ma has no idea that her children did EdgeWalk together. She thinks this photo is one of those fake carnival ones, where you wear a costume and pay twenty dollars for the photo. Looking at our brave moment up close again leaves me breathless. I haven't felt fearless since that day.

"You'd like Lauren," I say to Sierra's photo, as if she's here with me again. "She's strong-minded like you were. And funny, too. I know it's soon, but there's something unique about her. This could be it, *Princesa*."

I gently return the frame to my bedside table and lie on my back, eyes to the ceiling. Sierra would be nineteen now. I wonder if she'd still put up with me calling her princess. I wonder if she'd even let me hang with her like we used to on Saturdays, going to matinees and the skatepark, or if she'd be off with a boyfriend, instead. I close my eyes and swallow the pain. My heart, my throat aches with the memories I'm trying to push away. They return in a flood, along with the tears that stream down my cheeks, onto my pillow.

After letting myself relive the pain again for the first time in ages, I sit up, wipe my face with both palms and exhale. Lauren. It's almost noon. Should I wait a while longer? With my shift coming up, it might get forgotten. I can't be that guy who asks for the number and then never texts.

I find her in my phone's contacts, punch in her number and start typing.

<Hey. It's Sam. I'd love to see you again. We'll avoid flooded bars. Maybe a movie? Are you free one night this week?>

There. That's a start.
Here's to walking on the edge once more.

"Samuel. You input the progress report for Mr. Blakely, but you forgot to have me co-sign it."

"Right." I sigh. "I'll remember next time. Promise."

"Next time doesn't exist in emergencies. Remember that." Jake, the third-year resident I'm working with scowls at me, taps on a tablet, hands it back with furrowed eyebrows, then hurries off to the west wing elevator. I know this is my last warning. I've had a bad start working under him, and I could tell by his body language all day that he doesn't think I deserve to be here.

But I know that I deserve to be here. Just because I don't come from a long line of rich fathers who graduated from TFU Med, just because I don't live in a sweet little King Street condo or drive a new Audi doesn't mean I don't belong in this Med program. I may not look like the majority. I may not act like them. I definitely don't dance like them. But I can tie an interlocking continuous stitch better than any of them. We aren't even allowed to do it yet, but I've been practicing on a body at home. Not a real body. I hope I didn't mumble that out loud. Thankfully, every other student on the floor is rushing past me, as we all do, hour after hour, as we try to make a name for ourselves in this program, in this hospital.

Damn, I'm exhausted.

Once inside the empty change room, I open my locker, pull off my scrub top and change into a clean white shirt and jeans. I'll shower at home if I don't fall into bed first. My phone is sitting on the top shelf, so I grab it and sit on the bench between the lockers to read my texts.

There's only one:

<Flooded bar sounds fun but u have the wrong number>

I smile at first, thinking Lauren is flirting with me, but rereading it, reality sinks in. This isn't Lauren's number. I must have punched in the wrong digits when I saved her to my contacts the other night. I can't believe how daft I can be sometimes. Maybe I ate paint chips as a kid. I want to kick the locker, but knowing my luck, Jake will walk in just as I get into the really good kicking.

Maybe I can relieve some frustration tonight by practicing my IC stitch on that prosthetic foot at the back of my closet. There's another thing Ma has no idea about, and I hope she never finds out. Not that the foot is creepy, although, finding it would be an unpleasant surprise for my parents. But I wonder if they realize how not-normal I am. Normal guys my age spend their free time drinking beer and watching porn. Me? I suture a fake foot.

I toss my phone in my backpack and head for home.

As I pull out of the parking lot and slowly drive down Bangor street to our house on Johnson, I'm hit with a revelation every fiber of my being wants to ignore:

What if Lauren gave me the wrong number on purpose?

# 6: THE WAY OUT IS THROUGH THE DOOR. OR MASS EMAIL.

## SAM

I've always been a night owl, to my mother's great dismay. When I was in primary school, she'd try to make me tired by letting my sister and I play out in the backyard after our supper. She was always surprised to find Sierra practically putting herself to bed at eight o'clock while I was still running around the yard past nine, usually chasing a squirrel or dissecting a garden worm.

Now, it's my hospital schedule and class work that keep me up late, but if I weren't in Med school, I know I'd still find some excuse to be up when our house and street are silent and the streetlights have dimmed. I love going out for a walk at dawn to soak in that early morning hush. I enjoy knowing that I could be the first person in the city to hear the mourning doves coo. I love that lack of sound that happens just before the construction trucks on Nelson Street begin their annoying horn orchestra, before the garbage truck and school bus wheels start screeching like rusty grocery carts at every corner.

My early morning walk is another secret I've managed to keep from my parents, thanks to the back-door entrance that leads down to the basement. I hate keeping things from them, but they'd only lose sleep over it—especially Ma. Ma feels that the world is a hostile place, full of criminals and terrorists lurking in the shadows of every neighborhood. Pa wants double locks on our doors. I don't blame them after Sierra's gruesome murder, but now that we've moved from where it happened, I'm desperately trying not to live with that kind of fear. I'm not sure I'm succeeding. I manage to go for my early morning walks, but I don't like being out when dusk falls. Not late at night, just dusk. Sierra was mowed down at dusk. I'm also avoiding the kinds of adventures I used to leap at. It's partly my full schedule and mostly that I don't have anyone as special as Sierra anymore to join me. I could try asking one of my classmates, but I'm still finding my way with them. So far, I feel like such an outcast because I'm not a big partier. I have to pretend to be someone I'm not with them. What's the point?

I tried dating Shelley from my microbiology class last year but it only lasted two weeks. The entire relationship exhausted me because I spent most of the time trying to decide if I should text her or give her space. Even when she texted me first, I found myself reading between the lines, wondering what this exclamation point or that emoji meant. Should I send her a winky face, or would she think I was just being sarcastic? We only saw each other about three times, and I loved our in-person interactions, but the texting nearly destroyed my soul. It felt like I was on Survivor, and texting was like searching for the Idol and coming up short every time.

Believing I needed technology's wisdom in finding a match, I tried using Tinder last week and completely regret it. Jake had told me about how great it was for meeting women; I didn't realize until it was too late that it's more of a hookup app. I don't want a one-night stand. *Buen Dios*, I don't even want a two-night stand! I'm looking for someone to spend the rest of my life with. I suppose typing that up front to the girl, Dana, made me sound like a weenie because she said she'd meet me, and then she stood me up. I thought women wanted honest, solid gentlemen these days. #Metoo as a movement was needed, especially for the workplace. I just feel off-balance lately, as we all do, I'm sure. Is smiling at a stranger even okay anymore? I don't bother using Snapchat or Twitter. That would mess my brain up bigtime. Sometimes I just want to time travel years into the future, to a time when men and women have figured one another out, to a time when respect comes first over money and power.

The desk lamp beside me flickers as if it's laughing at my Utopian daydreams, and I have to smack it to get it working again. Stitch over, under once more, pull up. I'm suturing my feelings of stupidity and frustration away, practicing my interlocking suture for what feels like the 400th time. As I try to stifle a yawn that nearly reaches my eyebrows, I decide I shouldn't go for my walk at dawn tomorrow. It's past ten. I'll need more sleep than usual because of the long hours I just put in at the hospital. Feeling hot and realizing I need to get to bed, I pull off my white dress shirt and toss it aside.

"Son. Can I have a word?" It's my father knocking loudly at my door, and once again, I'm shirtless. I'm not sure how I managed to teach him this North American custom of knocking before entering a room. Everyone else in this family just breezes in like it's their room, too. My older Cuban cousins still live in Toronto, and whenever they visit, they sprawl across my bed, glued to their iPhones unless they need something to drink or eat, and then they ask me for it without even looking up. Like it's a five-star hotel, and I'm the bell boy. I guess they're used to five-star hotels; my father's brother owns a large furniture store that hotels frequent to decorate celebrity penthouses in the city. Those boys love to gloat about their wealth and success. I hate my cousins.

I place the prosthetic foot I'm working on down on the newspaper that's lining my desk. There's nowhere to hide it. He'll just have to deal with his son's strange obsession with stitching up fake feet. Ma might faint; he'll be fine.

"Sure, come on in," I say, turning my swivel-chair to face the door. He smiles when his eyes catch mine, then gives me a perplexed look when he sees the foot.

"Ah. My son the foot surgeon." He grins as he picks up the foot, brings it close to his eyes and carefully studies the suture. I'm not sure he knows I want to be an emergency surgeon, or if either of my parents heard me when I announced it. They very likely blocked it out. Pa's interest tonight

41

is surprising considering how little my parents have asked me about my studies over the years.

They aren't in this with me 100 percent, so they don't dare ask anything. I think they're afraid that I'll fail, and it will crush all of our hearts even more, if that's even possible. I try not to feel offended that they have such little faith in me and my ability to learn. It's not about me. It's about Sierra, about her absence in our lives—that enormous, gaping hole in our hearts that we've been unable to fill. Perhaps we've all been reluctant to fill it.

"Pa, have a seat." I gesture to the bed, and he puts the foot back on my desk, pushes my shirt aside and sits down. I swivel toward him and lean back. "What's up?"

"What's up is you've been declining your mother's invitations for dinner for the last few weeks. That's not the Cuban way. That's not our way." He furrows his brow, then sighs.

"We live in Canada, Pa. We have for a long time now."

"Canadians don't eat meals together?" He's always been argumentative, just like Ma.

"Yes of course. I just..." I sigh and motion to the foot behind me. "I have so much to do for school. I need to get better. I need to excel at this, Pa." I plead at him with my eyes. He doesn't understand.

"You were home and didn't come up. It hurt her feelings."

I can't tell him how much it hurts to sit there without Sierra and to see it in Ma's eyes—in all of our eyes.

"My hours are long, and I'm tired. But I will try to have more meals with you. Okay?"

"Bring a friend." It's the first time he's ever said anything like this. He's picked up the photo of me and Sierra at my bedside and is staring at it, looking teary-eyed and pensive. I inhale, taken aback, then let out a breath of relief.

"You and Ma have become so distrusting of everyone since..." I pause. "I didn't think I could ever bring anyone but family home."

"You can now. Our landlord, he says this is a good city. Very little crime. No terrorists."

"You're wrong," I say, hoping my defiance won't send him out the door. "It's everywhere. Good and evil, it's everywhere. We have to live our lives, or they win."

He looks in my eyes with an intensity I haven't seen since Sierra's funeral. His brown eyes are full of love, anger and fear all at once.

"We do have to live our lives. Yes." He exhales deeply, like he's finally going to allow himself this, for the first time in five years. "You have a friend at school?"

I stand up and sit beside him on the bed. "I met a girl, actually. Lauren. I really like her. But she gave me the wrong number."

"Ha! Oldest trick in the book! She is, what did that article say? Ghosting you." He smirks. I give his shoulder a little shove with mine, and he pushes back.

"I don't think so. I think it was a mistake. We connected. I think I may have typed her number in wrong, or she may have given me the wrong number by mistake."

"You don't know friend-zoned when it's in yo face!" He's chuckling hard, holding his belly. I'm impressed with his lingo, even if it does sound awkward with his Cuban accent. I think he's been watching YouTubers.

"I truly think we had a unique first meeting, and that she wanted to see me again." I hesitate, wondering how much an old man who spent most of his life in another country can really help me. But I'm desperate. "Do you have any idea how I can find her? She lives on campus, somewhere in Desie Hall."

His laughter has died down. He looks at me.

"You really like her? Then go after her! Go to Desie Hall. Kiss the girl!" His eyes sparkle.

"Pa." I shake my head. "In your day, that was called romantic. Today that's called stalking. It's not recommended."

His eyes widen. "What? How do boys ever get the girl? You can't knock on her door and present her with chocolates anymore?"

"She'd probably think I was a creep trying to poison her."

"So, slip a note under the door."

"The school would probably have to check that for anthrax." Now I'm just making stuff up, but he needs to know what it's like out there.

"Wait for her to leave Desie, then follow her to class!" He grins, proud of himself.

"Cringey-dude. Stalker-boy. I'd be hashtagged for life."

"Hash-tagged? What is this? A new sport?"

"No, Pa, but sometimes it feels like one." I stand up, feeling exhausted. This conversation is getting me nowhere.

"I know." He stands with me and starts for the door, then turns and looks at me. "But remember this: Any love worth winning is worth working for."

"So, you're saying I need to find her, win her love?"

"I know very little about kids today, romance today, technology today, but Samuel, love has not changed. It's still love. And love finds a way. Even if that's writing every Lauren in Desie Hall and having the letters checked for... anniethrax!" He leans against the door frame, beaming.

That's it! "Anthrax," I correct him. "I was joking, but you've given me an idea. Thank-you."

"We'll see you at supper tomorrow night?"

I open my laptop on my desk and check my schedule for the week. "I work tomorrow, into Tuesday morning, but I should be able to make it Tuesday night. If you'll let me sleep at the table..." I smile.

"I will bring you a pillow," he says, and leaves the room.

So, Pa gave me an idea. I'm going to try this. If I type in "Lauren" in the university email system, will it find several options?

> To: <Lauren Keough> <Lauren Fader> <Lauren Cuthbertson> <Lauren Rasula, Ph.D.> <Dr. Lauren Jolly, Department of Canadian Studies>

... and there are 241 more like that!

Woah. This should work. I should probably delete the Ph.D.'s and any name that appears to be a professor. Damn it won't let me. It will only let me keep adding Lauren names. This is a dumb idea. Should I keep doing this?
Why not? What do I have to lose?
It's a little bit crazy. Right?
But we had such a connection.
Dios strike me down, I'm doing this.

> Subject: Met you last night and you gave me the wrong number
>
> Hi.
>
> This is a mass email to all the Laurens at this university.
>
> If you don't fit this description, then just ignore this email. If you are the one I'm looking for, and you just don't want to talk to me, that's okay, too.
>
> If your name is Lauren and you're from England and you think Nietzsche is depressing, please text me at 613-548-6111.
>
> I'm Sam, by the way, the Med student who took you and your friend home after we were showered with beer on

**Friday night.**

This is nuts! I slam my laptop closed.

Buggernuts is what she's going to say to this email. I should delete it. I'm being a hopeless romantic in a world that locks people away for just looking at a girl the wrong way. I should delete this and try to forget about her.

I open my laptop and look for the composition page, but it's not there. I can't find the email anywhere. I search in several folders...

Sent.

It's been sent.

*Santo Dios Misericordioso*, what have I done?

# 7: DING DONG THE WITCH IS... UNDER MY CONTROL.

## LAUREN

I walk into my residence room to find four giggling girls crowded around my floor-length wall mirror. One is checking out what I assume are brand new thigh-high boots. The others are trying to convince her to wear them out tonight. I close my eyes for half a second, trying to wish myself into the parallel universe where I was granted a single room.

It doesn't work. When I open my eyes again, the redhead at the mirror is drenching hairspray on her straightened hair, her brunette friend's bun, and squirting it all over the textbooks on my desk in the process.

"Hey. Those boots look bangin'," I say, stifling a cough as I try my best to make them warm up to me after Brittany and the Bed Incident. The entire floor heard about that and for some reason I came out the whiny loser while she gained new friends. I'm not sure why I even want them to like me. They're not my type of people anyway, but I don't want to feel this lonely anymore.

"Yeah, I know, right?" The purple-haired girl in the boots—I think her name is Hailey—doesn't even look at me as she says it. She's still inspecting her thighs and admiring her butt in the mirror. Brittany puts her straightener down on my desk, places her arm around Hailey's shoulder and turns her cell phone toward the mirror.

"Move bitch," she says, and I turn to look at her two girlfriends sitting on my bed, like they're her posse and it's an inside joke. They stare back at me. Right. It's not a joke.

"Oh, me?" I fumble with my leather jacket, pull it off, toss it on the bed, and sit at the very edge.

"Yeah, you. Couldn't you see we were taking a selfie?" Brittany's mouth extends upward into a beautiful smirk of a smile as she snaps the shot. Then she turns and glares at me.

"We're kind of having a party in here." She grabs a beer from on top of her dresser and sips it.

"On a Monday night?" I ask in an incredulous tone.

"Yeah, sorry if we aren't all smart like you, but we don't want to waste our university years studying."

"Right." I bite my lower lip and straighten my plaid skirt. I don't have another response to that. When I signed up for this exchange and administration wrote they'd try to pick an adequate match of a roommate for me, did I miss the small print that said: dumber than the backside of a mule?

"So, can you like, leave?" Just as she says it, the Hailey girl bursts out laughing. She's sitting on Brittany's bed, so the other girls promptly leave mine and all three of them huddle around her. They're reading what I can only assume is some incredible piece of breaking news on Hailey's cell phone.

"He's a creep fo shore!" Hailey laughs and looks at her friends.

"I think it's romantic. Like out of a movie." Brittany flutters her eyelashes, swooning.

"Should we all pretend to be the Real Lauren, and send him, like, hundreds of ridiculous emails?" the redhead in black lipstick asks.

"No, no, one of the Laurens set up this closed Facebook group to chat with him, see? We can't get in though, without a Lauren."

This is surreal. I feel like I'm here, but not here. Am I suddenly a celebrity? Ha! That's hilarious; I've only ever been famous for my annual lemonade stand in my childhood years back on Bristol road.

What's going on here? I read about fame from a famous person's perspective recently; that the whole atmosphere of the room changes when a famous person walks in, and people talk about them like they're not even there. These girls are just a bunch of bubble heads, but I feel invisible like that right now, and I need to know why.

"Um." I clear my throat and stare at them, completely confused. "I'm a Lauren, remember?"

"Oh! I totally forgot!" Brittany opens her eyes wide, stands up, twirls in a kind of delirious glee, and sits beside me, tapping my thigh in what I can only assume is fake affection. "You *are* a Lauren. So, did you get into the Facebook group?"

"What's it like in there?" Hailey is sitting at my other side now. She giggles and beams at me like I've just married Prince William and might be the future Queen. "Like a sorority, right? I'm so jealous." Then she takes her gold brush and starts grooming the back of my hair.

"Allow that!" I say, grabbing the brush from her hand. Her eyes widen, and she sits back, arms crossed.

I raise my voice a little. I can't help it. "I have no idea what the bloody hell any of you are talking about!"

"You don't have to have a hissy fit about it!" Brittany sulks. She takes a deep breath and starts to explain as Hailey brushes the back of her hair. "Ok. Like, there was this guy who emailed over two hundred women named Lauren to try to find the right Lauren? The one who was at a bar with him that sprayed beer on them? Are you the Real Lauren?" She leans into me, and her posse does exactly the same.

"Uh..." Woah. Sam did that? He actually did that to find me? It's romantic and somewhat creepy all at once. But I know he's not a creep. What was he even thinking?

I look down at my lap and take a deep breath as I try to digest this overwhelming story. Do I tell Brittany the truth? I can't trust her as far as the ends of her fake eyelashes, but I do want to hear from Sam again.

I'll have the power in this relationship if I tell her. Maybe I can finally enjoy my room again. "I think I fit that description, yes."

"Omigod!" Hailey squeals. "He's so into you!" She grabs hold of my arm like it's a designer purse.

"So?" I say. "I mean, it matters if I'm into him too, right?" I shake off her arm, kick off my ankle boots and sit back against the wall. "Can I see this email you're going on about?"

"You didn't get it?" Brittany asks. "I wonder why? Jess from my psych class forwarded it to me this afternoon. It's gone viral." She grabs her phone from her dresser and hands it to me. That's a first. So, she likes me now. Seems it really is all in a name.

"Maybe because I'm an exchange student? I haven't received my university email yet. I'm still using my Gmail account."

The redhead laughs. "Oh! So, he emailed all those Laurens and not one of them was the right one, but now the whole university has seen it! Total Fail!"

I look down at Brittany's inbox and open the one with the subject line:

**Met you last night and you gave me the wrong number**

That first line, right there, I don't get that. I don't understand why he got the wrong number. Buggernuts. Could I have given him the wrong one? I've only had this phone for a week. Maybe I did. He must have thought I did it on purpose. Well, no, he didn't, because he decided to email me anyway. Along with 245 other women.

That's where this gets weird. What the hell? Who does that? I feel my neck and cheeks grow hot, and the tiny hairs on my arms slowly raise, but it's not because I'm spooked. Rather, I'm flattered.

Who does that, indeed? Who goes to that extreme just to talk with me again? No one, ever.

I read on:

If your name is Lauren and you're from England and you think Nietzsche is depressing, please text me at 613-548-6111.

"He remembered our conversation about Nietzsche." I feel the warmth of that memory surge from my heart up my neck to my cheeks. If anything, I need to see Sam again to get my textbook back. I realized on Sunday that he kept it by accident on Friday night. Plus, he's smokin' hot, and I haven't been able to stop thinking about him holding up that umbrella for me. Not for days. Who'd have thought a dead philosopher and unexpected beer showers could spark a romance?

"Who's Nietsky?"

Did I say that out loud? Bugger. "Just a philos... never mind. I want to text him back." I grab my phone from my rucksack at the door and start to open my text messages.

"*No.*" Brittany grabs the phone from my hand and places it under one of her butt cheeks. "First, you have to get us into that Facebook group."

"How can you get in? You aren't a Lauren."

"No, but you are. We want to look at it through your account. If we're going to stay popular at Desie Hall, we need to be in-the-know about all of this." She tosses her straight blonde hair over her left shoulder and throws a cunning look at Hailey, who's nodding in eager agreement like a kindergartner on her first day. "So, that means you have to meet The Laurens at the café tonight. Jess who knows Kendra who knows Lauren Johnson in third year told me where they're meeting."

I sigh at the thought of it: a room full of Laurens. I just want to get into my pjs. I have a ton of reading to do. "Can't I just request to join?"

"Lauren says she's vetting everyone to make sure fake accounts aren't accepted. You'll have to do it in person."

"I don't have to do anything of the sort." I make a face and get up to change. "I don't need to meet any more Laurens. One of me is quite enough, thanks." I chuckle at my own joke.

"I'll start behaving," Brittany says quickly, getting up with me.

"Yeah, we won't have room parties without asking anymore!" Hailey adds.

I didn't realize she knew it was inconveniencing me. She's brighter than I thought. I do want to text Sam and sort this whole thing out, but I suppose I should meet the women who've created a whole Facebook Group because of me. Besides, I've been telling myself I don't feel lonely here, but I do. Maybe this is the answer.

I turn to Brittany. "You'll let me sleep in on Saturdays? No alarms, no phone calls until ten?"

I can't expect her to stop inviting people to shag on my bed. That's going to take years of behavioral modification and even then, she'll probably shag her therapist. But getting back my Saturday mornings? That's a start.

"I'll let you sleep in, and when you Skype your boyfriend with terrible fashion sense, I'll leave you alone," she says smugly.

"Lexy isn't my boyfriend. She's my dearest friend, and I think her outfits are bangin' so shut your mouth."

"Wasn't she a he?" She scrunches up her nose.

"Yup. Does it matter?"

"I guess not..." She twirls a strand of hair between two fingers and continues scrunching her nose, gathering her pea-sized thoughts. "I've just never met a Transvestite before."

"Transgender." I correct her, desperately trying not to roll my eyes. I want my quiet Saturdays. "And it's an adjective, not a noun. She's a transwoman."

"Sure, I already knew that," she fibs.

"Right. So, we have a deal."

"Oh goody!" Brittany squeals, clapping her hands together.

"Now for the important part," she says to her posse, and I feel my heart flutter, believing for a split second that she wants me to lead a book-club-like discussion on how I met Sam—on what makes him tick, on how difficult it is to meet good men these days. Instead, she opens my closet.

"What are you going to wear?"

Heather Grace Stewart

# 8: WILL THE REAL LAUREN PLEASE STAND SO WE CAN KICK YOU INTO SUBMISSION?

## LAUREN

"Hurry up, it's pissin' rain and getting cold out here," Brittany commands her posse.

As we stand on the wet, leaf-covered sidewalk in front of Starry Night Café waiting for the others to exit the car, I notice our Uber driver checking out Hailey's legs in her black stiletto heels. I'm not surprised: every one of these ladies including Brittany is what I call "Look At Me! Hot." They always wear outfits that accentuate their boobs and show off their toned legs.

I'm not saying there's anything wrong with that. Women should be able to wear whatever we damn well want after a century of mandatory corsets and petticoats and blouses buttoned up to our necks. I just can't be arsed to put on makeup and a sexy outfit every time I leave my residence room. I love my yoga pants and trainers far too much, so that's what I wore here. Brittany was nonplussed when I told her I would put on some makeup, but that I was staying in cozy clothes.

"Don't you want to look your best?" she asked with a more perplexed look on her face than usual.

"Sure, but why does my best have to include makeup and heels?"

"It's just what everyone does in all the top magazines."

"Right. I'll remember that next time," I replied, too knackered to argue this one. I hope they have English Breakfast tea and scones. It's all I'm craving, and besides, the coffee at these places is dodgy. They're all students working here and appear much too busy flirting with one another to clean the machines properly.

"You're our ticket in here, after you." Brittany giggles as she opens the glass door for me. I sense unusual nervousness in her laugh. I hope it's not such an exclusive club already that these four can't join the table.

Starry Night café is bright, very warm and smells of tangerines and mulled cider and spices. I take a few steps inside, unzip my jacket and pull off my gloves, then take a look around. There are brightly painted square paintings on the red brick walls with little cream tags under them. I glance at the closest ones and notice most of the paintings are by local artists. All I see are splashes of paint with abstract shapes, which I've never much liked, but I smile when I recognize the large Van Gogh print for which the café is named on the brick wall behind the coffee bar. *Starry Night,* with its bright blues and yellow hues, has always made me feel peaceful.

The dozen or so tables are all full except for a small one at the back. Everyone seems to have either a large mug of coffee with milk froth and a cinnamon stick in it or a glass of wine. Some are digging into large slices of pie or cheesecake. I turn back to Brittany.

"That must be them; it's the largest group," I say, and everyone follows me as I head to the long rectangular table at the back of the room. A group of women are sipping tea and coffee, chattering and laughing as if they're the only ones in the room. Most of them seem to be our age with the exception of a woman who looks like she's in her early forties.

As I approach the table, I notice someone has made a makeshift cardboard sign for the table:

**#Laurenfromlastnight**

It makes me want to laugh out loud and quietly retreat all at once. How do I explain myself? Where do I begin? I've never been in a situation like this.

It's too late to leave. I have about fifteen pairs of eyes on me, and the silence is deafening.

"Hey. I'm Lauren Green. I'm actually..."

"She's the Real Lauren!" Brittany squeals beside me, clapping her red gloved hands together. "She knows Sam and everything!" I hear a slow but intense intake of air, like she's just announced Meghan Markle is here to do makeovers for every one of them. As the women exhale and start reacting to the news with giggles and whispers, one woman stands and shakes my hand.

"Lauren Johnson, third year Engineering. This is just... it's just hilarious. We're all happy to meet you. We've been wondering all day who the Real Lauren is and how we should reply to Sam." She grabs a metal-backed chair from an empty table behind her and pulls it up for me to join them. Brittany and the others keep standing, looking rather awkward.

"I came with them." I smile. "They're on my floor."

"But it's a Laurenfromlastnight Club," Lauren says, her lips pursed. I cannot believe this.

"It's that exclusive?" I say incredulously. "They can't stay for coffee?"

"Are their names Lauren?" A redhead in a navy-blue beret says this like she's tasting bitter espresso with a spoonful of snark. She's about three Laurens down and one across from Lauren Johnson. This is just weird. Now they're my Lauren Landmarks. It's the only way I can make sense of them all.

"Now wait everyone, hold on just a second," Lauren J. says to the group, then turns to look Brittany up and down. "I suppose we can make an exception this time, since you brought us the Real Lauren, but you can't be in the group photo. Sit at that table behind us," she says.

Brittany, Hailey and Jenna take off their coats and, like the losing team on *Survivor,* sheepishly scuffle over to their designated Tribal Council spots.

"This time?" I ask, looking up and down the table at what I now count as sixteen women, seventeen including me. "What do you mean?" I place my gloves and small purse on top of the menu since I just want black tea.

"Oh, we've been bonding today, sister! Who cares about Sam,

we've got our own Facebook group, and it's Lauren-powered! We're going to be meeting every week," a brunette Lauren explains in a booming voice.

"Yeah, I created the Facebook group," Lauren J. adds. "It's closed, but here, punch in your name and number as Real Lauren in my contacts, and I'll let you join."

I take her phone and think on this for a second. Sixteen new friends named Lauren. I could use friends in this city... but sixteen with the same name? That's ludicrous.

"Smile!" someone says, and I look up from the phone to find Lauren J. snapping a group photo. "This is legendary!" She laughs. I hope she doesn't tag me. I like my privacy. I'll have to ask her to leave the tagging out of it for me.

*Crash!* My thoughts are interrupted by a plate or more smashing to the floor, followed by shouting. Some poor soul just lost their job in the back room. *Shhhhut!* Milk is being steamed and frothed behind the coffee bar, dishes clatter as the waitress collects them, and the Leonard Cohen song coming through the speakers is at the part where he's remembering Heather's legs all white from the winter.

The noise level at our table, however, has fallen to a hush. The Laurens are silently watching me as I punch in my not-so-original name. I decide to give them my full name, number and Gmail not so much out of wanting to belong, but so that once the Laurens accept me into their exclusive club, Brittany and her posse will leave me alone again. Most of all, they'll leave me alone on Saturday mornings. Ahhhhh, I can already feel the comforter warm on my face as I sleep in next Saturday. I hand the phone back to Lauren J., wave down the waitress and order a tea. When the waitress leaves, I look back down the table to find the women all having private conversations, so I take the silverware in front of me and start scratching at my napkin with my fork. What can I say? Social anxiety at its finest.

"Can you explain about the being showered with beer part of Sam's letter? And the Nietzsche?" Lauren J. finally asks, and I stop murdering my napkin for a second. Do I have to tell them that story? It's mine.

"Gosh, well, first, could you ladies please tell me if you answered Sam yet?"

"Of course not; it wasn't meant for us. Didn't you answer him yet?"

"I didn't get the email."

There's another audible intake of breath. Call Hollywood, I have all the audience sound effects needed for their next hit talk show.

"But... why?" Lauren J. takes a sip of her white wine and purses her lips as she looks at me. "He emailed two hundred and forty-six of us. You know that, right?"

"Yeah, I heard about that from my roommate. I didn't actually get the email. I think it's because I'm an exchange student. I'm not yet in the system."

"Wow." Snarky Lauren leans her large chest over the center of the table so I can see her face. She'd been hidden beside brunette Lauren. "If you think about it then, it's thanks to us that you're even here. We created all the buzz." She smirks.

"I suppose so..." I say. "I would have heard one way or another, I'm sure."

"Like on Twitter, tonight." Lauren J. grins at everyone, and they all nod. I've missed something.

"What?"

"Nothing, I just want to share the story tonight, with our photo. No biggie."

"Oh, please don't. I haven't even spoken with Sam yet!"

"So?" snarky Lauren says. "He involved all of us when he emailed half a country."

"Yeah. What he did was totally stalkerish if you ask me," a blonde Lauren at the end of the table says, stirring her café latte.

Lauren J. interrupts and takes over, a pattern I'm beginning to notice. "We were talking before you arrived. We don't think you should answer him directly. You can talk to him through us."

"You think he's stalkerish? No! He's the sweetest, most clever, dreamiest..." I have to stop myself. This isn't Lex I'm speaking with! I hardly know these women, and besides, Brittany and Hailey are leaning in, like they want more deets to share with the floor. I don't owe them anything.

"We don't know for sure, do we? Maybe he was just being romantic, but as we've all been taught, we should play it safe. For now, I can email him what you want to say." She places her hand over mine, like sealing a pact I haven't yet made. "That way he can't reach you directly." The other ladies nod in agreement. I look down at my tea, feeling like a child being told that I have to eat all my peas before I can touch dessert.

"I... I mean... do you think he's dangerous... could he really be?" I pour a little cream in my tea and give it a stir. I can't believe this. They have me questioning Sam's character. He's one of the good guys! Isn't he? I spent two hours with him on Friday night, and he was kind enough to get me and Boozy Brittany home safely.

"Who knows?" Lauren J. answers. "Just don't answer his email and don't meet him by yourself."

I take a sip of bloody awful cold tea and mentally run through my red flag checklist, feeling the eyes of nineteen women boring into my brain as I think. There were no red flags, and I got to know him! I found out what he's studying here (emergency medicine), where he's originally from (Cuba)... the music he likes (uh, I think he liked the live band)... shite.

I don't really know much about Sam at all. He knows far more about me. Buggeritall. He knows where I live! Maybe the Laurens are right.

Maybe I spent Friday night with a stalker.

60

## 9: EVERY PRINCE HAS A FEW HICCUPS

## SAM

"Catch."

My classmate, Ronny, throws me a clean scrub shirt, and it lands on my head. It's soft and smells like fabric softener, so for half a second, I forget how this place reeks like the janitor's just washed the halls with bleach and Ben-Gay.

"Thanks. I can't believe I did that." I pull off my coffee-covered green scrub shirt and toss it in the bottom of my locker, then throw my empty coffee cup in the garbage. I only got two sips; what a waste of an overpriced mochaccino.

It's just a scheduling coincidence, but Ronny and I often pull shifts together. I like him enough, although he's competitive. He told me he wants to finish first in the class, and nothing would stop him from reaching that goal. I'm surprised he's willing to loan me this shirt.

"Just be glad we aren't in our surgery rotation yet. You'd be late by now." Ronny slams his locker shut and leaves the room as I pull on my fresh scrubs. There it is. The jab. The undercut punch. Everyone here does it. I'm surprised he didn't say it in front of Jake (I've got to remember to call him "Dr. Marshal" in front of patients), the resident who's marking us on our performance in inpatient care today.

I close my locker and let out a loud sigh. What Ronny doesn't know won't hurt me. I already spoke with Jake and got my instructions for the morning. That's how I ended up with coffee all over my shirt, when an eager student wheeling a patient out of their room too quickly bashed into me. I'd see it as a bad omen for the day, except today, I get to work with people, and not ones in cardiac arrest or surgery, but people I can joke around with while I check their vitals. I don't have to stand back and observe; I get to jump right in and participate in patient care. I like days like this.

As I enter my first patient's room, Jake's already there with Ronny. The man in the bed won't stop hiccupping. Jake is asking him if he smokes or drinks or if he's ever had a hernia operation. I stand near the far wall and observe, then pull out my tablet to take notes.

"Mr. Henry Goldberg has tried all the usual treatments for hiccups, but they just won't go away," Jake explains to us. "His physical exam was unremarkable. Diagnosis?"

Ronny jumps in before I can open my mouth, shoving his tablet under Jake's nose. "He had hip replacement surgery here a couple days ago, it's on his chart, right? Wouldn't surgery cause hiccups?"

"That's what I'm thinking. Good call, Ron. I'm going to give him an antipsychotic, Thorazine, which should stop the problem altogether."

Ronny is nodding and looking proud of himself. I'm still taking notes.

"So, we'll keep him for observation?" Ronny asks as Dr. Marshal injects Thorazine into Henry Goldberg's arm.

The patient suddenly hiccups so loudly, Dr. Marshal nearly trips backward. I manage to stifle a laugh, but Ronny doesn't succeed. In fact, both he and Jake are biting their lips and looking at each other, obviously finding this whole scene like some wonderful inside joke.

Just when I think the patient is going to rip them apart for their disrespect, he smiles at them. "They're gone! They're gone!" Jake just nods, a smug look on his face.

"Watch him until noon, then release him this afternoon. That was when he was set to be released." He looks at me. "I'll leave that to you. Ron, you can follow me to my next patient's room." Ron follows on Jake's heels like a loyal Labrador retriever.

So that's how today's going to be. Ron gets to observe with Jake, and I'm stuck with Hiccupping Henry. I look at the man sitting up in bed, blanket pulled up to his abdomen, take the cold, metal seat against the wall, and reread the notes I took on this odd case. Dr. Marshal says it's cut and dry, but something isn't sitting right in my gut.

I wish I could check my email and see if Lauren has responded yet, but I can't do that until my break in an hour. It's already been a day, and... nothing. I hope she didn't mind the mass email. It was one of those brave moments, like walking the CN tower edge with Sierra, only in this case, I kind of regret it now. I wanted to be romantic—to show her what a great time I felt we had on Friday night, but maybe it seemed desperate. I should have waited for her to come out of Desie Hall one morning, then pretended to bump into her, but the idea of that just felt stalkerish.

No, I did the right thing. I wanted to find her, and I let her know. Along with 245 other women. I counted yesterday, after I found the email in my Sent box. I sent that email to a lot of Laurens. Only one has responded: "Not me." A Lauren Johnson. No other replies.

I love the convenience of texts and emails but miss the emotional journey that happens with snail mail. You take the time to choose the stationary, the pen, the stamps; you decide what you want to write and compose your letter. Pa tells me that in days gone by women would spray it with perfume, then use a wax sealer. You'd send it off and await a reply. The planning of the letter and anticipation of the reply was all part of the enjoyment. It reminds me of good patient care, actually. All that thought and effort directed at one person!

Romance was dying a slow death with email and got murdered when texting came along. Those kissy emojis look like they're having a coronary while chewing bubble gum. The hugs are so rosy-cheeked, they look like they're constipated, or taking a crap.

I smile at the idea of sending Lauren a handwritten letter. Maybe she'd be happy to receive an old-fashioned gesture like that. Maybe she'd even save every letter that I sent. Tie them up in a red satin bow and hide them in a box under her bed.

"Hic, hic. *Hic!*"

I'm pulled out of my daydream by Hiccupping Henry. He was trying to read Sports Illustrated, but his hiccups are so bad again, the magazine is bouncing up and down on his large beer belly.

"*Hic!*" He puts the magazine down after this brief, not-silent struggle and rolls his eyes.

"They're back," I say. "Are you feeling okay?" I ask.

He shrugs, then lays back in bed. No, not lays, he's sliding down, unable to sit up anymore, and his legs are jerking like they have a mind of their own. I think back to what I've studied in Pharm. Side effects of Thorazine? I'm not allowed to manage this unsupervised, so I press the call button to get Dr. Marshal and some nurses here.

Before they arrive, I quickly check Henry's blood pressure. It's dropped to a dangerous level; I shift the bed, so his head is lower than his heart. The nurse comes in, sees what I'm doing, and gives me a hand. I'm itching to give Henry some saline solution to bring up his blood pressure, but I need to wait for my resident. As soon as he's here, I'm telling him what I believe is going on. No more compliance; timidity doesn't make for a good doctor.

"What happened?" Jake's arrived, with Ronny in tow.

"Blood pressure is eighty over sixty. Possibly a side effect of..."

"Yup, it's just the meds," Ronny chimes in.

"I don't think so," I interrupt him and turn to Jake, who's already administering saline solution. "Dr. Marshal, Henry's low blood pressure is a common side effect of Thorazine, but we should order blood tests to rule out infection or an abnormality."

"Good. Done." He's impressed, but he's not going to give me more than that.

"I was going to say that," Ronny says. He's standing beside Jake while I'm arranging the patient's bed so he's more comfortable. The nurse checks his blood pressure. It's returned to normal, but now he's moaning along with the hiccups. Ron leaves to order the tests, and Jake asks the nurse to stay and observe the patient's vitals. As we leave the room together, he pulls me aside in the hallway.

"I need to show you something. Come to the break room; it's empty right now."

I can't figure out from his tone what I've done, but he doesn't sound happy. We sit on the grey sofa in the dark and dismal break room (there's never been a budget for this space), and he shows me his phone. It's on Twitter.

"You want me to see your tweet?" I ask incredulously.

"It's not mine. It's the Top Trending tweet this morning. It's about a Sam Sanchez emailing two hundred and forty-six women to find the love of his life. Or something like that."

I feel my heart bursting out of my eyeballs. He hands me the phone so I can tap the tweet and read the attached article. It's from BuzzFeed. It's definitely about me. How did they get my... Oh... My name. Of course. My name was attached to my email. But how did this get out? Why? Who would share this on social media?

"Twitter is going batshit crazy over this. Is this you, Sam?"

I nod quietly, then meet his eyes. "I didn't mean for it to be a big thing. I just wanted to find her."

"Well, it's a big fucking thing now. It's already on twelve news sites that I can count. Local and national. These guys... they're relentless. They'll be at the hospital asking questions soon."

I hadn't thought about that. Hell, I hadn't thought anything. It was all my heart.

"Am I in trouble?"

"You aren't. You're the guy who's nuts about her. You wanted this. But what if she didn't want this?"

"Her name's out there? Jake, I don't even know her last name! How could they?" I grab the phone back and study the article closely.

"Whoever tweeted the photo of the group of girls. She created the hashtag #laurenfromlastnight, and it's trending. Your Lauren's name isn't released on Twitter yet, or in the next article, but these news people will want that scoop. They'll want to talk to her. They won't back down. And then they'll want to turn you into a creep." He looks at me intently. "Which you're not. You're a pain in my ass, but you're no creep."

"You sound like you're speaking from experience," I say, my voice trembling on the last word.

"My Dad's a journalist. I've watched him work himself into a frenzy since I was a kid, and I watched him retire and start writing books because he didn't like the dirty rules of the game anymore. Sam, don't even question it. They *will* find her, and they *will* harass her."

My heart sinks to the floor. I want to puke. "I won't let them. I won't talk."

He shakes his head. "We'll do what we can, Buddy. What were you thinking?"

I see empathy in his eyes, and for the first time ever, I feel like we understand each other. I have no answer for him.

"Come on, let's go to HR, then Security." He takes back his phone and stands up.

"They all need to be notified, and you need to be prepped." He makes his way to the door. "At least we caught it before they got here. This whole thing has blown up fast."

I stand up quickly. *Buen Dios.* "Oh my God."

"What? You're only realizing what a train wreck this is *now*?" He stops at the door and stares at me.

"No. Things blowing up fast... Jake! It's an embolism. Henry Goldberg. He's got a pulmonary embolism."

# 10: UP A FOLEY'S CATHETER WITHOUT A PADDLE

## SAM

Jake hasn't admitted he thinks I'm right—the day that happens is the day Donald Trump admits he rolls around in Doritos—but I know he at least thinks I'm onto something. I know this because without saying one word, we've started jogging side by side down the hospital corridor to Henry Goldberg's room. I'd like to pick up the pace and sprint like the man's life depends on it, but even in emergencies, hallway running is frowned upon. We still make it to his room in record time.

We find our patient lying on his back trying to rest, eyes closed, the Sports Illustrated rising and falling on his belly every time he takes a breath. Or, to be more exact, every time he hiccups.

"Mr. Goldberg," Jake says softly, "we need to examine you again."

The nurse beside the bed gently taps him on the shoulder. He opens his eyes and nods at us.

"Hic. Hic. *Hic*" That poor man.

Jake pulls back the blanket and examines his arms and legs. "There's shortness of breath, but no redness or swelling. What do you think?" he says, looking directly at me. He's actually asking my opinion. I'm dumbfounded. I pull him outside of the room for a private conference.

"Dr. Marshal." I detect a smirk on his smug face as I begin my analysis. He hasn't been taking me seriously for months, but maybe now he will. Maybe this is my chance. "While there's no swelling, we've both noted that there is chest pain present and a racing heartbeat. What made me think of a pulmonary embolism is, I remembered hearing about a patient in the Toronto Western ER with persistent hiccups. Turned out she had a blood clot in the lungs. It was fatal." I emphasize that last word as I look down at my notes on my tablet to make sure I've covered everything. Jake looks at me for half a second, and I think he's going to completely blow me off. Then the nurse comes out of the room, and he grabs her at the elbow.

"We need a CT of the chest, stat," he says. He turns back to me and gives me a quick pat on the shoulder.

"He's a relatively healthy guy, Samuel. I doubt something as rare as a PE is going on in his chest, but you know what, this could be a good learning exercise for all you rookies. We'll have the CT results in an hour. If it checks out fine, we can give him more Thorazine and send him on his way. He's taking up bed space."

"Did you seriously just say that?" I stare at him in disbelief. Jake's an arrogant womanizer. He's never been the kind of man that I respect, but I've always respected his work as a doctor. "Aren't we taught to respect our patients?"

He looks up from his tablet and glares back at me.

"Sam, don't you have other patients to check on? Get to it."

"Yes, Doctor." I'm learning more than techniques every day. I just learned where a line is drawn. I can come up with a diagnosis for one of his patients, but I can't tell him how to treat them. I look down at my tablet, find my next patient's name, and rush off to her room. I feel an incessant vibration inside my pocket and know by the nonstop buzzing that it's #laurenfromlastnight related, but I don't have even half a second to check my phone.

I don't have much time to feel anything when I'm working and learning at the hospital. I don't have time to put any more energy into Henry Goldberg's situation, and I certainly can't think about how Lauren might be feeling or the media shitstorm that's coming. All I can think about is the patient I'm with right now, and when I enter Jan Leggett's room and check her tubes while she's sleeping, I notice right away that something's off. Jan's Foley bag, which was collecting urine from the catheter in her bladder, is empty, but it shouldn't be. I check to see if the bag has recently been changed. It hasn't. My heart leaps into my throat, and my palms grow sweaty.

I may be in the early stages of my training, but all of us know that poor urine output is never a good sign. What am I supposed to do? Think, Sam, think. I need to find my patient's nurse right away.

I step outside the room and nearly run into Julie; the short, bustling, dark-haired nurse in her forties who's assigned to Mr. Goldberg. I ask if she has a minute and give her the lowdown. Her eyes are kind as she explains to me what's going on. "The Foley catheter is just kinked, honey, blocking urine from emptying into the bag. All we have to do is re-insert the Foley. Easy peasy!" She smiles up at me. I appreciate her not making me feel stupid. As we walk back to my patient's room together, I replay her instructions in my head. Sure, just re-insert the Foley. You bet. I can totally do that! How the hell do I do that again?

"You're wondering how all that awful shit can go down, people sick and dying, when it's such a peaceful night out there, eh?"

The giant of a night janitor (I swear he's Hagrid's Canadian cousin) stops sweeping the locker room for a moment. He scratches his full, dark beard and stretches his arms over his head as he awaits my response. I just nod. It's about all I can manage after such a draining shift. He's caught me in a rare moment of repose, staring out the one window in this dark and stuffy locker room. Despite the city lights and pollution, I can still see a few stars twinkling in the sky. It did seem tranquil out there, and I was wondering how that could be. We lost two patients tonight. I wasn't involved, but I heard about them from Ronny. As for Mr. Goldberg? He's going to be alright, it seems, but only because I caught it in the nick of time. A few hours later and he certainly would have died from the blood clot lodged in his lungs.

"Samuel." Jake pulled me aside in the hallway a few hours ago. I'd just finished learning how to put in a fresh Foley catheter, thanks to nurse Helen and her extreme patience. "Results are back from the pervasive hiccups."

I hate how hardly anyone here refers to the patients by their name, but instead calls them by their symptoms or diagnosis. I know some day I'll probably have so many patients and be so overwhelmed with their cases and my surgeries that I'll forget to call them by name, but I hope not. I hope I remember to stay human. It's why I wanted to become a doctor; it's what my sister would have wanted. I studied Jake's expression. He's always hard to read, but today, it was obvious from the look in his eyes that he was feeling remorseful and slightly embarrassed.

"You got it right. It's a PE. Kudos to you for figuring it out." He cleared his throat and looked down at his tablet. I wasn't going to get a public congratulations, but that's okay with me. This was enough. This was the fuel I needed for the rest of this semester. When things go wrong, as they always do here at ECGH, I will have this moment to keep me going.

Wait. I'd just saved a life! I needed more. I deserved more than one lousy, "Kudos!" I stood there staring into space and imagined a sweaty Freddie Mercury right behind me, belting out "We are the Champions" in tight black leather pants as the Dean of Medicine, donning his black cap and full blue and red academic dress, hand-delivered me a beautiful, yellowed scroll with gold embossed words at its centre:

**You're A Winner. You belong here.**

"Samuel. Are you even paying attention?"

Jake's low voice pulled me from my daydream, so Freddie's song and the academic pomp and circumstance came to a full stop. Nooo! Damn. That was one short moment of glory. You can't get five fecking minutes of fame around here!

Instantly, I heard my sister's voice in my head, "Get over yourself, Sam. It's not about you. It's about the sick people." She was always the bossy one.

I snapped myself out of my daydream completely and gave my full attention to Jake. "I want you to work with his nurse for the rest of the night," he said. "Put him on blood thinners. I've sent you a few recommendations, so check your email. The patient will have to be on this for three months to prevent additional pulmonary clots."

"I'm considering writing a paper on this case." He furrows his brows. "It's curious to me. Could hiccups actually be indicative of a pulmonary embolism?"

I nodded, unsure of where he was going with this. Was he asking me if I would co-author the paper? I'm not a resident yet. But surely, since I made the correct diagnosis, I'd get my name on this paper?

"That's all. Dismissed." He kept looking down at his tablet, waving me off with one hand. So much for my name in lights.

I pull on a clean white shirt and blue jeans, give my hair a quick brush, stuff my tablet in my backpack, and pull my phone out of my scrubs' pocket. I forgot about all that vibrating I heard earlier. I saw about a dozen new personal emails when I checked my tablet for Jake's case recommendations—I really need to get two different emails: one for med school and one for my private life—but don't have time to read them.

The same ones are sent to my phone, so as I saunter down the near-empty hall, I start scrolling through them.

> **Subject:** WTF Sam?
>
> **From:** My oldest cousin.

So nosy. I'll get to him later.

> **Subject:** How come your name is on TV news
>
> **From:** Carlos Sanchez

My father. Shit.

> **Subject:** Your Mass Email
>
> **From:** Lauren Johnson

This one could lead me to Lauren. I keep reading.

> I'm not the Lauren you want, but I met her the other night. We've formed a bond. There is a group of us on Facebook, and we want to protect her because we are divided 50-50 on whether what you did was slightly stalkerish or totally romantic.
>
> I can let you speak with her. You can send her email messages through me. She won't meet you alone.

I glance up for a moment, trying to make sense of something nonsensical and realize I've just nearly tripped over one very old man. He's bald and half blind (Seriously. I'm not kidding. There's a patch on his left eye.). He's sitting in a wheelchair to the right of the hospital's front glass doors.

"Crazy kids! Coulda killed me! Always glued to your phones! You know what I should do with that phone? *Shove it up your asshole!* That's what!" he shouts and shakes his fist at me, then turns his wheelchair in the opposite direction.

Huh. So much for polite Canadians.

"I'm sorry!" I call after him, letting the asshole comment slide. I did nearly land in the old man's lap, after all. Just as I'm about to chase after him and explain about my bad day, maybe buy him a coffee, I hear my name. Not just once. Several times.

"Sam! Look here! Sam!"

I turn to the group of voices and have to blink. There's a storm of flashing lights, a steady click-click-click of cameras, and too much shouting.

"Sam! Are you going out on a date with Lauren soon?" A tall, white-haired reporter leans in close and shoves a small black digital recorder under my face.

I duck away from the three reporters gathered around me, feeling like a boxer in a fight. I dash toward the doors and manage to swing through them fine but have to halt just outside. Another half dozen men and women are standing there, calling my name.

"Why use email? Why didn't you just text her?"

"Can you confirm Lauren's last name?"

Damn. Jake and I never found a minute to tell Security or HR about the situation, and then we completely forgot. Now it's too late.

I look to my right. There's a red and white TV truck parked at the corner. I look ahead. A sea of frenzied reporters, standing on the leaf-covered pavement, shouting my name. There's only one way out, along the wet cobblestone path to my left. It goes behind the hospital, and there's that alley that leads to the lakeshore that I'm sure they won't know about. I pull off my backpack, cover my face with it, and make a run for it. They don't chase after me, at least, not on foot. I smell smoke from someone's backyard fire pit, now just wet cinders in the rain, as I sprint behind a stretch of old homes.

A few minutes later, I reach Valentine park and the stunning aluminum alloy "Parallel Worlds" sculpture. I've passed by this sculpture, built by artist Rami Gold for Edwin Cove's Tercentenary, many times while going for a run along the lake. I've also taken breaks here to reflect and study. I've heard several stories from my fellow TFU students—some on drunken nights but also some from completely sober students and even one professor—that the sculpture is a working time machine. If only! If I could only disappear into the sculpture and turn back time to one week ago. Damn, I'd do things differently. If I hadn't sent that mass email, maybe I'd be having a coffee in a cozy café with Lauren tonight, not running from this pack of wolves.

I glance over my shoulder once more. There are no suspicious looking trucks following me, and only one couple walking hand in hand on the path ahead of me. Sprinting along Lake Ontario, then up Fifth and Grand streets in near pitch-black darkness and cold autumn rain; my wandering way lit only by a few antique streetlamps, I run through everything leading up to today's events in my mind. Lauren and I enjoying the live band together, then laughing as the beer tank exploded and showered us. Lauren and I carrying Brittany up the steps together. The look on her face as she gave me her number. It was positive, I remember that. She wanted me to text. Everything that's happened since then... *Dios*... everything is spiraling out of control!

She'll never forgive me. Maybe I wanted my five minutes of fame, but not like this. Never like this.

Oh, Lauren, I hope you're safe.

# 11. HELL-O, YOU ARE HERE. <<<WHERE YOU DON'T WANT TO BE.

## LAUREN

I wake to two chords chiming: a notification sound called "Hello" in my iPhone.

It sounds like a distant church bell at first, but as I slowly come out of deep sleep and the chords keep chiming, I realize that it's not sacred or enchanting. It's annoying. Like a drill hitting steel, over and over again:

*Hell-O*

*Hell-O Hell-O.* I thought it was a sweet sound when I first chose it. It was kind of cute: "Hello, you've got an email." "This will pick up your day and make it so much brighter." Now it reminds me of a small child tugging at your pantleg again and again and again until you pick them up.

*Hell-O Hell-O Hell-O Hell-O Hell-O!*

"Buggernuts! Who in bloody hell is that?" I feel around my bedside table for my cell phone and pick it up, accidentally knocking a book onto the floor in the process.

I rub my eyes and look at my cell phone. It's not one person. It's about forty new notifications coming in! How is that even possible?

"I hate when I forget to put my phone on night mode!" I say to Brittany, who's not even here. Where is she?

Sitting up in bed, I look at my cell closer and check the time. 7:45. I don't have a class until eight-thirty, and it's just one street over. I could have slept some more, buggeritall. I hate when my sleep is needlessly interrupted.

Over seven hundred notifications in total. I don't know where to begin. I've never been needed this much. A far second place would be when One Direction broke up. I had to turn my phone off for a couple of days because all of my besties were having breakdowns. I open and read the first email:

**To:** Lauren Green lgreen0618@gmail.com

**From:** Braden Price bprice@EdwinCoveGlobe.ca

Hi Lauren. I'm Braden from The Edwin Cove Globe. You're very popular on Twitter. Yours is such a sweet story that our readers need to know more about it. Have you made a date with Sam Sanchez yet?"

"Very popular" on Twitter? I have fourteen followers, what is this wily wanker even talking about? I open my Twitter app and check my notifications there. Oh. My. Buggeritall. I have 1,818 new followers since I last checked this two days ago. For half a second, I feel the thrill of fame run through my veins. My heart's aflutter. I'm famous!

Wait a second. I don't want to be famous for this. They know I'm *the* Lauren, the one Sam was trying to find. How did they find out? How? This is why my email is blowing up. They've talked to some of my Twitter followers, and now they've got my email address.

I stand to leave, thinking maybe I need to speak to someone in residence security, when Brittany bounces in, beaming at me with those winter white teeth. Lordy. I'm rooming with Miss Winterfest Parade. She's in her pink and white workout gear and doesn't seem the least bit out of breath, but by the tiny beads of sweat on her forehead I can tell that she's just finished her morning jog.

"Brittany." I cut to the chase. I hope she'll be able to follow me better this way. "Which one of you gave my email address away? My phone is blowing up!" I hold up my phone close to her face. "When I go on Twitter, my name is trending under Trump. I don't know if I should scream or throw up. I'm quite sure I'm about to do both."

Brittany shrugs her shoulders and turns to look at herself in the mirror. She pulls out her ponytail elastic, rolls it onto her wrist, and starts brushing her long tresses.

"Lauren J. tweeted a few words about laurenfromlastnight as a hashtag, and then I guess she spoke to a reporter or someone in her DMs, and they tweeted a bloggy thing? Then that bloggy thing was retweeted one thousand one hundred and seventeen times, isn't that coolio?" She pauses to look at my reaction in the mirror. "And then this morning, some guy beside an EC-TV truck pulled me aside and asked me what your last name was. He was so hot... he only looked about ten years older than me, so I thought I'd give him my cell number."

"You're dating a television reporter."

"Not dating, silly!" She giggles. "I'll probably just let him feel me up." She turns back to the mirror.

I sense last night's dinner rising up inside my GI tract. I'm definitely going to puke. I sit at the foot of my bed and put my head between my legs.

"So, like, before I said I had to go, he asked me if I knew you, and I said I'd seen you around here. No big deal. I mean, they can't find you. There are so many Laurens involved in this thing!"

I can't see her anymore, but her voice is shrill and nasally, and it's starting to get on my nerves. I take a breath and look up again. She's sweaty, and yet somehow, she sparkles in a way that's still beautiful. Now I know why men desire her. If she can look good this early in the morning and after five-kilometer run, of course they want her by their side. And other places.

I've always tried to be unique: the shimmering snowflake each one of us was born to be, and yet here Brittany stands, looking like every other cookie-cutter girl on this residence floor, and she's getting all of the attention from boys, and older men, which if you asked me is rather creepy. I just don't get why unique isn't special anymore. Instead, it's considered strange. Why does society do its very best to make standing out undesirable?

"Lauren, why are you staring at me like that? Do I have sweat under my boobs?" She flaps her shirt back and forth, air drying it. "I hate that under-boobs sweat so much, don't you? Take a picture of me now okay?" She hands me her phone. "And I'll pretend that I'm all embarrassed to look so gross, that would be too cute right?" She giggles and grabs her towel off its hook behind the door, then poses with the white towel against her cheek. I presume she has to think for a minute about how to find her way to the showers. I stand in front of her so she can't leave and stare at her without taking a photo. She grabs the phone back from me and sighs, clearly annoyed, pushes past me, and opens our door.

"They have my email address, Brittany!" I raise my voice. Why does it feel like I'm her mother instead of her roommate? "Now they could have my room number too."

"Okay, that must have been Lauren J. I didn't give your dorm room number out. I wasn't that stoopid!" Brittany whines, and stomps her foot. For a millisecond, she looks like an angry horse, and I'm happy.

"You said I was at Desie Hall!"

"I said I'd seen you around. But, I mean, there's gotta be hundreds of Laurens living here right?"

"They are journalists. Trained journalists! They'll follow you to me!" I throw my arms up in the air in exasperation. She opens the door wider and starts to leave, then turns and rolls her eyes at me.

"You overreact to everything. If you want to make any friends, you're going to have to start acting like everybody else." She gives me a frown, more like a pout that I'm not falling into line like the rest of her posse, then briskly leaves for the showers.

I'm about to check my weather app to decide what I should wear today (I heard from Hank who's visited here before that I should be bracing myself for six-foot snowbanks by month's end. I'm not sure if he was kidding or not) and realize there's quite a ruckus outside. I'm not hearing the usual morning noises, like car doors slamming or students greeting one another as they walk to their classes. These are loud, anxious voices, and they're calling my name:

"Lauren, are you in there?"

"Lauren from last night, come outside!"

I look out the window and can't believe what I see below. There are at least half a dozen reporters with microphones in hand, and two television trucks parked right in front of Desie Hall. They're all here for me. Buggernuts. This is unbelievable. I wonder if they've found Sam as well.

I sit down on my bed and try to remember to breathe. Why am I so bloody worried about him at this moment in time? My very safety is in jeopardy, and I'm thinking about Sexy-with-a Cherry-on-Top Sam Sanchez. He's the one to blame for all of this, and here I am, imagining him without a shirt. Mmm. And oh, there we go, now he's pantless. I'm shameless.

Lauren. Take a deep breath to try to forget Sexy Sam. Remember how he put me in this terrible position.

Ahh, that smells wonderful. Someone is making toast and brewing coffee down the hall. I see that Brittany left the door ajar, as usual. There are loud giggles coming from next door, and I'm hearing the strangest sound: Velcro tearing, very slowly.

Giggler one: "Are those tear-away pants?"

Giggler two: "Damn straight. Got them on sale!"

Giggler three: "So cool! Put them back on. I want to rip your pants off!"

Giggler one: "As long as I can tear your top off."

Ew. I close my door, so I won't hear anything else. That was weird. Tearaway pants? I actually live here, in this place where conversations like that take place all the time. I would be giggling myself, except I have the small concern of half a basketball roster waiting to interview me outside.

I look down at my phone. There are still hundreds of notifications I don't have time to check. I'm supposed to be in class in twenty minutes, but I don't feel safe enough to leave this building. I'm going to have to cut class for the first time *ever.*

Damn you, Sam Sanchez!

Just as I think it, an email with Sam's name hits the top of my inbox. He found my email, too. Should I even read it? Won't it make me angrier?

I take a deep breath and decide to open it.

Lauren:

Lauren Johnston agreed to give me this email address and told me you'd agreed to meet with me, with all the Laurens present, at the Starry Night Café tonight at 8 p.m.

I am profusely sorry for how all of this has turned out. I never meant to hurt you or embarrass you. I hope you're safe and with family and friends right now. I will understand if you never want to see me again, but I wish I had a chance to see you face to face, to discuss why I did what I did, and to apologize in person. If you're willing to meet me in a more private environment at the café tonight, can you come by at 7 p.m. instead? The media and the Laurens won't find us there at that time. Just a thought. If you want, I'll send for an Uber to pick you up at 6:45.

Wishing for a fresh start,

Sam

I read his email twice. This doesn't sound like a stalker. This sounds like Sam. He sounds like the guy I liked. He's concerned for me and deeply sorry. Why did I listen to the Laurens? Maybe if I'd met with Sam earlier, I wouldn't have reporters hounding me at my residence!

I peer out the window again, careful to just look through the sheers for a second, so no one sees me up here. I'm going to have to talk to Lauren J. about all of this at the group meeting tonight... that is, if I can find a safe way out of this room. I have beef with that girl, and I'll give her a piece of my mind! I'm willing to bet she published that photo of all the Laurens at the café, despite that I asked her to leave me out of this. If I'm remembering it clearly, she took the photo. She's the most to blame for this ballsed-up mess of a media circus.

Opening Twitter, I scroll through tweets with the hashtag #laurenfromlastnight. There's been so much activity and retweeting in just a few hours, it's hard to find the culprit who started it all, but it appears that one of the Lauren accounts dished on everything to a popular blogger, who in turn told the whole world about Sam's bold move. Yeah. It was a bold move, a little crazy-stupid, maybe, but I know in my heart that he had good intentions.

As I read the hundreds of tweets from dozens of different countries, I'm blown away by how everyone tweeting about this is acting like this story is theirs to tell. Yes, Sam made it public domain when he mass-emailed so many women at the university. But was it really their story to share? I haven't even responded to his email yet, and it feels like the whole bloody world has read it! That lousy crew of Laurentuplets are to blame, and yet they told me they'd protect me from Sam? How is any of this protecting me?

I feel warm tears on my cheek and wipe them away with the back of my pajama sleeve, then swallow hard to hold back the rest. I don't want anyone here to see me crying, but I'm scared, and I feel more alone than I ever have in my life. I wish Lexy lived in this residence, so I could run to her room and feel safe once more. I wish I was back in Coventry. I'm going to leave campus as soon as I can get in touch with Hank. Hank will give me the money to fly home, or maybe he'll even let me stay with him and Béa in France for the rest of this semester. It's a shame, because I was starting to love my studies here. Even Nietzsche was growing on me—just a little, mind you.

Glancing out the window once more, I see a man in a grey coat with large, dark eyes staring up at me. Suddenly, I can't breathe. I wanted to start a bold new adventure here, to try living outside of my box. Instead I feel more boxed-in than ever.

# 12: LATE BLOOMERS

## SAM

"Here. Take these. Late blooming fall flowers. It's like you and love, Sam." Pa gives me a firm pat on the back and tries to hand me a small bouquet of bright orange and purple asters from our side garden. I think he was probably picking them for Ma until I told him about my maybe-date at the café in half an hour. I'm at the fridge drinking a glass of milk in an attempt to calm my nervous stomach. It's been flipping around like a gymnast on the pommel horse since my last email exchange with Lauren. My apology went over better than expected, because she finally gave me her cell number. Her *actual* cell number. We're getting somewhere!

"Thanks, but I'm not even sure if Lauren's going to meet me. She kind of left it up in the air after I said I'd send her an Uber."

"Why not bring her flowers? Pick her up like a gentleman?" Pa asks, sniffing his quaint bouquet. He looks offended that I don't want it.

"It's complicated. I didn't want to overwhelm her," I say, closing the fridge.

"Is she a good woman?" Ma's standing in the kitchen door, leaning against the doorframe.

"I think so. I really think so." I rinse my milk glass, put it in the dishwasher, and turn to look at her.

"You bring her here for Thanksgiving. Then, we will see. Only then." She looks over at Pa, and they share a look I can't quite decipher. Years of marriage breeds its own language.

"I really messed things up with her," I say. "With all of those Laurens. They have the wrong impression about me. I'm not sure she'd come, but I'd love to ask." I give Ma a kiss on the cheek. Ma and Pa know all about the mass email—they wouldn't let me go to sleep until I explained everything last night—but they both insist that it was romantic. Of course, they would think that. Their first date was at a church dance. They still believe courtship should be an experience, like a fancy five-course meal, not the fifteen minutes of swiping and tapping that so many of us make it today.

"You made a mess of things? Before you even got started? You give the girl my black bean Cuban soup. Is comfort food. Better than flowers," Ma says as she hands me a large, clear Tupperware container filled with soup that smells of fragrant black beans, cumin and onions. I stare down at the container in my hands. Ma's cooking is always delicious, but I don't think this is the right gift for Lauren.

"Thanks Ma, but soup isn't a first date kind of gift. More like a fortieth anniversary meal."

Pa is smirking at my mother. "Monika," he says, stretching the i in her name out as he always does when he doesn't agree with her, so it sounds like Moneeeeka. "You and your big batches of soup. We will have soup until February first."

"Yes, and that's good! It saves money! I can freeze it."

Pa looks out the window. "We have money. Much money. The crowdfunding money." He doesn't look at either of us.

"Carlos. I will never touch that money. You know this. Is pity money. Evil Muslim terrorist money."

"Ma," I interject. "We don't know that it was terrorism. Probably just terror. He was mentally ill."

"He was Muslim terrorist." My parents say in unison.

"There are many more mentally ill people who need help in this country than there are terrorists." I turn away from them and walk to the coat closet. I can't get into this, not now and hopefully not ever again.

The day of Sierra's death, people started tweeting about the van attacker being jihadi before they even knew his name. My family are immigrants, so it surprised me that they immediately fell in line as well, screaming about how Muslims are taking over Toronto.

"Pa," I tried to reason with him a week or so later when I thought that, because they were all cried out, they were also all screamed out (they weren't). "Not all Muslims are terrorists! When people panic, in person and online, about how dangerous Muslims are, it totally distracts us from the real problem behind mass killings."

"You know what the real problem is, my son who goes to university? Tell us." Pa shouted at me. He sounded angry, but his tired eyes were brimming with sadness. Ma was sitting beside him, staring into space. I wanted to reach out and pull her close, stroke her long hair, let her cry into my chest. She hadn't done any of this, not even at Sierra's funeral. She never cried in our presence. Stoicism was her default position.

"Hateful online communities and male violence. It's a lethal mixture."

My parents said nothing in reply. They just looked down at their laps. Finally, Ma spoke.

"Maybe it's the Internet. Maybe that makes more violence. But those people..." she shook her head back and forth several times. "Those people are dangerous."

I wasn't about to remind her how most people see Cuban immigrants. I wasn't going to start throwing out statistics about which community was seen in a better light. I just wished they would remember that we came to this country to try to live in peace, as I know many Muslim families do.

Despite my parents stubborn, racist stance, to my surprise they were willing to attend the #TorontoStrong crowdfunding benefit concert that September, six months after Sierra was killed. The concert was to support the victims and their families, first responders and those affected by trauma. We had been packing up our house to move to Edwin Cove. Ma had told Pa she needed to "get away from here." She couldn't handle being reminded of the van attack every time she went anywhere near Yonge street.

"What should I bring? To feed the officers there?" she asked, and I remember staring at her like she'd lost her mind, which I fully expected to happen earlier, right after we lost our Sierra. It had taken six months.

"It's a benefit concert, for us, Ma. We just bring us."

"But it's such a chilly night. I should bring something for officers, first responders in the crowd. They'll be hungry. I know! I'll bring my Cuban black bean soup."

Later, we were getting in my truck, and sure enough, she handed me a huge silver pot of soup before climbing into the back seat. It was a solemn occasion, and yet I found myself chuckling out loud. "Ma, you don't need to serve soup!"

"But they might be hungry. It's cold, and they're working long shifts."

I saw flashes of Sierra's heart sail across my mother's eyes and said no more about the soup. It ended up being a big hit at the concert and somehow broke the ice for us, making our entrance less awkward than it may have been. As indie bands played melodic songs on stage, people waved their lighters in the air and gathered around us to get a taste of the black bean soup Pa was bragging about. Ma even served a bowl to a woman in a hijab. I wasn't sure if she realized her own hypocrisy. Were "those people" only dangerous after midnight? Or had she meant only the men? I certainly wasn't about to say anything. I took a mental photo of the moment instead, filing it away under "hope."

My mother and Sierra set the bar high. No matter what kind of pain they were holding inside of themselves, these two women were always putting others first. They were hard-headed and they interfered in almost every aspect of my life, but their hearts made up for all that. I want a woman like that by my side. Hopefully, though, she won't be quite so obsessed with soup.

86

"Flowers! Bring the flowers!" Pa shouts behind me, shoving the brilliant orange and purple bouquet into my hand. Stubborn man. I grab them out of respect.

"No flowers. They just wither and die. You give her my black bean Cuban soup." Ma calls from the kitchen. "If she's a good woman, she'll forgive you without flowers."

I don't have time, but I want to tell her that if I'm lucky enough to be forgiven, it will have nothing to do with Lauren being a practical person or an upstanding citizen and everything to do with how much one person can take from this media circus I've created.

Slipping on my jacket, I check my phone. I have five minutes to get there, but it takes fifteen. I lost track of time. Shit, I'm late. I'm late, and she's probably waiting at the café, wondering why she gave me a second chance.

I jump into my truck, throw the flowers on the passenger seat and the soup container on the floor, pull into reverse, and head down Johnson Street. *Dios.* For so long, I've been afraid to fall in love. Afraid to even put myself out there. Sierra's death tore my heart apart; one more heartbreak may stop it from working altogether. I may have a chance to feel real love with Lauren, to make my heart whole again, but here I am batting zero for two.

I try to imagine what my sister would say at this moment: "Stay calm, Sanchez. It's just the first half, and there's stoppage time." The thought of Sierra in my passenger seat, bouquet on her lap, rolling her eyes at me, makes me breathe easier. She's right. Baseball isn't my game anyway. I've always been better at basketball, a game of instinct and heart. What was it former President Barack Obama said about why he loves basketball? *"It's about building a team that's equal to more than the sum of its parts."*

<Ping.>

Could that be Lauren? I've just parked on Brock Street, which leaves me a five-minute walk to the Starry Night café.

I check the phone. It's her.

<Uber driver is honking for me out front of Desie, but too many journalists. Can't make it out safely>

What? This is insane. Why isn't the school or the police getting involved?

<Is there a side entrance?>

<Just checked, yes. Accessible entrance, east side of building, D wing.>

<Stay in your room for now. Will text u in 5>

I start the truck, pull off Brock and pray I don't hit any lights on my way to Desie Hall. I hit two and decide to run them. It's Sierra's fault. She's yabbering at me again:

*You get a second chance after all, Sanchez. DON'T. BLOW. IT.*

# 13: BLACK BEAN SOUP AND GINGERBREAD EARS

## LAUREN

I can't believe I'm bloody doing this. I'm all for living outside of my comfort zone, hell, that's why I moved here, but running straight into Sam's arms after the stunt that he pulled probably isn't the smartest move I've made recently. I know that the Laurens would agree, hell, they straight out told me not to see him without all of them present. They aren't the boss of me! But I do respect Lexy's opinion. Would Lexy agree?

Should I find out what she thinks about this ballsed-up mess? Doesn't matter, there's no time to Facetime her about my decision. Sam's just texted that he's at the side door.

I rush down the residence stairs to the accessible door, outside and straight along a short path to the passenger side of Sam's truck. I had no idea how to dress for the occasion, so I simply threw on the rugby shirt I got at the bar the night I met Sam—somehow it reminds me of happier times—a pair of dark jeggings, black runners and sunglasses, hoping that would help hide my face from any reporters skulking around the side entrance.

So far, there's no one here at all, but I'm still feeling incredibly anxious, especially because it's already dusk outside.

"Hey," I say as I open the door.

"Hey, back," Sam says. As I slip onto the passenger seat, my feet kick a book on the floor. "It's my Nietzsche textbook! Buggernuts, now I have to do my readings," I say, taking off my sunglasses and picking it up. "Thanks for remembering."

"I promised to return the book, and I keep my promises." He hands me a beautiful, fragrant bouquet of tiny wildflowers. I wonder what they're called.

"These are asters, from our side garden. I know it's not a good enough apology for all of this..." he gives me a sheepish, sideways smile, and I realize I'm staring into his eyes. I don't even want to look away. I know I'm supposed to be mad at him for putting me in danger, but just sitting near Sam makes me feel safe.

"Thank you, these are lovely." I give them a good whiff and exhale for the first time in what feels like hours. "I can't believe the crowd up front." I gesture behind us as he pulls away from Desie Hall. A couple of students have seen us, and they start laughing and running after the truck. People know what we look like? This is all too much.

"Keep me safe?" I ask in a near-whisper.

"That's why I'm here," he says.

"Two questions. One: Any idea where we're going?" I ask as the truck continues north along King Street. The sky is a cloud-filled deep purple, and there's a chill in the air. For the first time since I moved here, I notice the leaves on the trees starting to turn red. I can't wait to see the full effect in a few weeks. So many reasons to stay.

"As far from campus as possible because they expect us to be there. I was thinking we could go to the Putt N'Glow. You ever play glow in the dark mini-golf?"

"Not once!" I chuckle and look at him to see if he's serious. "But I'm up for it."

"You're in for a good time." He smiles. "What was your next question?"

I put the flowers and book down and hold up a clear container of what appears to be some kind of black bean chili. It smells heavenly, like my grandmother's kitchen, but I'm not sure what it is doing at my feet. "What's this?"

He blushes slightly, and I can see him trying to gather his words. "My mother thinks, you know, with all this reporter nonsense, that you could use some of her black bean soup." He glances at me, then turns his eyes back to Bathurst road. His cheeks have grown scarlet red. "Family recipe and all. I mean, we can dump it if you want, when we get there. She was insistent."

"We are not dumping this soup!" I keep it on my lap. It feels warm, like the rest of my body. "Your mother sounds like a wise woman. Tell me more."

He smiles at me with those lovely hazel eyes and starts telling me about his family. I think we may bloody drive off the road if he doesn't pay more attention. It's a good job I'm not driving because I'm lost in his eyes, too. They're spellbinding. Second only to those chocolate curls. Hot earlobes, too. What? He has sexy earlobes, okay? I don't know how else to say it. They look as though they were made to be nibbled like a gingerbread biscuit.

"Lauren."

"Hm?" Sam's at my door. I nearly drop the soup.

He opens the door for me and holds out one hand, chuckling. "It's fine, I daydream all the time. I just hope it was good."

Now it's my turn to blush. "Oh, it was. Or will be."

## 14: EVIL PIRATES ARE BANGIN'

## SAM

"You have the most adorable feet."

Lauren has accidentally pulled off a black sock along with her shoe, revealing her dainty left foot, delicate toes and toenails painted in the sexiest shade of deep purple I've ever seen.

The second the words leave my lips I want to hit myself on the head repeatedly with this mini putter. I wish I could retract the comment, but it's too late. Lauren glances up at me from the bench where she's sitting but takes her time slipping the sock back on her foot. I'm trying to lean on my putter like I'm calm and cool, but I'm absolutely not. One hundred percent Neanderthal. That would be me.

"And you have adorable socks." She smiles, shoving her shoes under the bench beside mine. There are only two other pairs of shoes there besides ours. It's a quiet, uncrowded night at the Putt N' Glow; our white noise being laughter, the happy pinging of arcade games and a catchy Michael Bublé tune spilling from the ceiling speakers. I can't complain about the atmosphere or the aroma. The place smells like cotton candy and fresh-popped popcorn. I'd believe I'd taken Lauren to a fair if not for the tacky pirate and crocodile statues at every corner.

"Got a thing for Harry Potter, do we?"

I look down at my dark grey and red socks again and lift and wiggle my feet to show the bottom of the socks off to Lauren. I didn't know I would be revealing my sock choices on the first date, but what the heck? This is supposed to be about getting to know each other better. Get real or go home.

93

Lauren starts chuckling as she reads them. The right sock says MASTER HAS GIVEN DOBBY A SOCK! The left one says DOBBY IS FREE!

"My Pa bought them for me. He loves reading almost as much as I do. I thought they were original," I say. I can feel my neck growing red.

"They certainly are," Lauren replies as she stands, putter in hand. "And that's coming from someone who lives in the UK. I thought I'd seen every piece of Potterware on the planet—twice."

"So, we'll start with golf, and then try laser tag if we feel up for it? Sorry about the angry pirates everywhere." I gesture around the large room. "It's not a four-star establishment."

"What? Evil pirates are bangin'! I especially like the one over here with a Dark and Stormy in his skeleton hand." Lauren chuckles as she walks over to the pirate skeleton statue at the start of the eighteen-hole course.

"Okay, so each hole is par three? Here, you forgot your 3D glasses." She hands me a pair of large blue and red 3D glasses to wear for the course. "Let's do this."

"Great." I take the glasses, look at her and bite my tongue. Don't say it, don't say it. I'm not about to tell her that she looks adorable in her 3D glasses, even though she does. Damn, she's beautiful. Even in the dark. It's not that dark, though, because everything's glowing. We now have larger-than-life, luminous pirate pals at every corner.

"You go first, since you've never done this before," I manage, still trying to adjust my eyes to the 3D glasses. I haven't played mini golf here in Edwin Cove, but I did play with my cousins back in Toronto. I'm looking forward to teaching her a thing or two about the game.

Lauren places the ball on the starting point, studies her three-dimensional pirate-themed surroundings, swings back and takes her first shot.

"Ha!"

One stroke, and she's pulled a trick shot, bouncing the ball off the side of the boat and into the pirate skeleton's eye sockets. I look at her in amazement.

"You've done this before!" I cross my arms over my chest.

"I bloody have not!" She looks offended, then starts to bite her lower lip and surreptitiously looks away. She's been having me on! "I've never done this." She's not looking at me, but I notice she's fluttering her lovely long eyelashes behind those glasses a few too many times.

I faux glare at her, place my ball on the starting point and take my shot. It lands on a lily pad in the pond, beside a glowing crocodile.

"Oh, bad luck!" Lauren is snickering.

I shake my head, putt the ball over to the skeleton's eye sockets and head to the next hole with a smile on my face, trying not to look like a poor loser.

The second I get there Lauren's already achieved her hole-in-one inside the treasure chest. She turns to look at my sulking face, puts one hand on my chest, throws back her head and laughs with me. Only, I'm not laughing anymore. My heart is racing at the feel of her soft hand grazing my left pec. Does she even realize she's touching me, or is this just a natural movement for her? She's standing so close to me I can feel her warm breath on my neck. She feels comfortable with me. I'm about to faint, and she feels comfortable.

I look down at her. "Something you maybe want to tell me? Like, you've played before?"

"Oh, is this confessional? I've already been this month, Sam, I'm good." She licks her upper lip, like she's just finished an ice cream, then bends down in front of me to place her ball at the next starting point. I can't think. I can't even remember what I'm doing here.

It's like she doesn't even have to try. She's already won.

95

"Whew. I'm a little sweaty!" I air out the front of my shirt as I say it. "That was quite a workout." I raise my glass to Lauren and take a long swig of root beer as she wraps her hands around a white teacup. I started to buy her a beer when she politely told me she wasn't big on cold drinks and would be perfectly happy with a hot cup of Earl Grey tea. It made me feel at ease just hearing her say that to me. No second guessing with this woman: she tells you like it is.

"Yea, me too. I won golf, but you kept finding me in laser tag, no matter where I hid. You're good!"

"I think we should try the vault next. That maze, where you try to avoid the laser beams?"

"Oh! Yes! Everyone else seems to have left, so we can pretend like we're spies." Lauren giggles. She's right; we're the last people here, but the place doesn't close for another hour. She puts down her cup and wipes a small bead of sweat off her forehead with the back of one hand. "I know it's immature, but..." She smiles at me and raises her shoulders, shrugging off the comment in sudden insecurity. "Never mind."

I reach across the table and take her hand. "You are far from immature. From what you told me on the way here, you moved all the way across the ocean after your parents split and your boyfriend transitioned. That was brave."

"I don't know, maybe I was running away from my problems..."

I look at my frosty mug, then shove it aside and take Lauren's other hand.

"I'm not sure this is first date stuff, but I hope we can keep seeing one another, and I'll have to tell you sometime."

"Tell me what?"

I take a deep breath. "My family moved here after my sister was killed by a man who drove into people on the sidewalk. He just... got into a van and drove into them." I breathe out, feeling a sense of relief that I've finally said it to someone who matters. I hadn't told anyone in the Cove yet, until now.

"Holy fuck." Lauren's not even blinking.

"Yeah, pretty much," I frown. "So, you could say we're running away from our problems, too. Moved away. But I think it's more like learning to manage the pain. Finding new ways to carry it around."

"Do you think you'll always carry it around?" She asks this softly.

I didn't expect this. Most people change the subject after I tell them how Sierra died. This is refreshing.

"I think so. I... I have a hard time walking outside at dusk. That's when the driver hit her. My parents are worse. They trust almost no one, and they're afraid to travel anywhere. Our lives are completely different. We don't look at the world the same way." I hear myself talking to her, and I want to get up and leave. I can't believe I'm sharing this much. I'm sure she'll never want to see me again after this. I exhale, trying to hold back my tears, so at least I don't cry in front of her.

"Let me tell you something." She looks right at me. "I had a hard time getting on the plane here from London. I was afraid, y'know... You always wonder these days. You just never know, with all the incidents lately. I had a good laugh with some folks working in security, and before boarding, I told myself that the world is generally a good place with a few pockets of evil. That's how I choose to see it. I think it's different for you because you lost someone you love. But you have to decide, do we live in a friendly universe, or a hostile universe?"

"I don't see it as hostile anymore, but I'm not a hundred percent sold on the friendly, either." I attempt to smile at her. "I hope the load gets lighter. Meeting you..." I don't know if I should finish that yet, so I don't.

"I know. I've never met anyone like you, Sam. It does make the load lighter." She finished my thought. *Santo Dios*, she's incredible.

"Uh, seriously? I made a colossal mess of things. There's a media circus outside Desie Hall, and you can't go on social media without seeing hashtagged stories about us."

She shakes her head. "Yes, what you did was something a crazy person would do, but in the end, I liked it! I liked how hard you tried to find me. It was a sweet, romantic gesture, you just went about it wrong." She squeezes my hand.

"At least you made some new friends."

"The Laurens? Are you fucking kidding me? They're a right piece of work." She rolls her eyes.

I make a loud "Pahh!" sound as I laugh out loud at her frankness, then dab my nose with a napkin to make sure there's no root beer dripping from it.

"Oh, do you think they leaked the story?"

"Think? I know. Lauren J. took the photo, and I asked her not to tag me, but she went ahead and opened her big hole on Twitter. Then my roommate essentially handed the reporters my dorm room key."

I grab my phone, fuming. "I'm calling the police. I'm sorry I didn't do that earlier. This is ridiculous."

"No, no, I already texted my father about it, and my brother, Hank. Hank's in security, so he knows what to do. They're contacting administration, then the police if necessary. I'm sure it will all be resolved by the time you drive me back to res. The emails I'm getting, well, that may take a while to fade to a dull roar, but I've turned off my phone for the time being."

"If those media maggots aren't gone when we get back, I'm standing outside your door the entire night. If they harass you, they should prepare to die."

She beams at me. "Thanks, Inigo Montoya, but I can take care of myself." I feel both turned on and amused to learn she speaks fluent movie references.

"I'm sure you can. Your golf game proved it. But are you up for laser-dodging, Lauren Bond?"

Her face lights up. "Sounds like fun. Let's go in together." She stands and walks towards the vault, then turns her head over her left shoulder.

"Oh, by the way... I told the truth. Never have done glow in the dark golf."

"I knew you were an honest Englishwoman."

"Right, but Dad's taken me golfing pretty much every week since I was three." She grins over her shoulder, takes one look at my expression, and makes a run for it as I chase her into the vault.

"Hang on, my eyes need to adjust to this lighting." I gently squeeze Lauren's hand to stop her from attempting to jump under the first laser beam. I was surprised when she took my hand once I caught up to her. I knew we'd connected today, but I wasn't sure if she was feeling friendship or something stronger, until now.

"Right, Gramps. I forgot you're older than me." She squeezes back, and I decide here and now to forfeit the game without her knowing. There is no way I can win at this when all I can think about is the electricity from her fingers touching mine, and how in this darkness, the vanilla-mandarin scent of her hair has grown more fragrant. It's intoxicating.

"I see seven beams now. Can we go through them together?" I ask.

"I've actually never done this before, but I set it to two players, so let's try." She gets down on her knees, ready to crawl under the first two beams.

I look down at her and chuckle. "Sure. Because you're always honest about whether you've done something before or not."

She doesn't respond. She's already making her way through the maze. "C'mon! You're gonna balls it up."

"Oh, sure blame the old guy," I call behind her. I try not to look at anything but the laser beams and how I should move my body to avoid them, but the woman is crawling on the floor in front of me, and she's wearing leggings. It's distracting.

We're almost there! I see one more beam, just to my right, if I can just stretch my leg this way and bend a little farther, I'll be able to narrowly miss...

"Damn!" I jump up and land standing beside Lauren as I reach the finish, but it's too late. The beam turns red. The machine beat us.

"Oh well," Lauren chuckles as she looks up at me, cast in red and orange light. Her face is glowing like a wrapped gift under the Christmas tree.

"Let's face it, we'd be crappy spies."

When our eyes lock, I grip her waist and pull her in closer. She's breathing rapidly but her heartbeat is far steadier than mine. I slowly bring my thumb to her bottom lip and caress it in small circles.

"I don't know, don't all great spies get the girl in the end?"

"Why can't the female spy get the guy? This is the twenty-first century." She lifts her chin and presses her lips to mine. Her mouth feels warm and sensual, and the kiss is far from timid. I don't want this to end.

I lose track of time and location. Our world is soft and silent except for the sound of us briefly coming up for air. Half a second later, our lips are pressed together again.

"Hey!" The laser vault attendant, who can't be much older than me, is behind us. "You two need to leave so others get their turn."

We pull apart, our eyes still locked. Lauren starts snickering.

"Hey, sorry. Thought we were the only ones left." We push through the black metal door and come into the light arm in arm, laughing.

"This is the best date I've ever had," Lauren says, and I couldn't agree more.

"But there's more." I remember the Big Wheel. "If you got a hole-in-one, you can spin the wheel and get your pick of a stuffed animal. You got several."

"This is bangin'! Let's go!" She hurries her pace. "I had my eyes on that purple dragon."

# 15: TRUST ISSUES

## LAUREN

"You sure you're okay to go in by yourself?"

Sam comes around to the passenger side of his truck and opens the door for me. It's quiet at my residence except for the constant humming of one flickering streetlight on the corner. I glance up at the faulty bulb. It's all that's lighting this side of the street, but I feel safe and content in the darkness with Sam by my side.

"Yeah, it's late. They're all gone, Sam. Don't worry about me." I take his hand, jump down from my seat, and let him pull me in closer to him. I don't want this date to end, but I've missed enough classes. I have to get up early tomorrow. I look down at my phone, ignoring the many notifications on the screen. 11:58 p.m.

"You'll be turning into a pumpkin soon?"

"Something like that." He lifts my chin and kisses me softly, but this time we don't have anyone waiting in a lineup to pull us apart. His lips taste sweet and his neck smells like those mahogany teakwood candles Lexy used to tease me for sniffing obsessively in the Bath & Bodyworks store.

"Oh. My. Ovaries. Smell this one! Leather. Teakwood. It smells just like... like...a sexy man!" I said, handing her the candle.

"Yeah, but it smells like a man who's a *player*." She emphasized that last word as she took another whiff.

103

"So bloody what, if he smells like *This?*" We burst out laughing and bought three candles.

I melt into Sam's teakwood scent, but he pulls back a little and sighs. "I should let you get some sleep. Oh, don't forget your winnings!" He opens the back door, reaches in and pulls out the googly-eyed purple dragon I won earlier along with my textbook, a slightly withering bouquet and his mother's soup.

"Thank you." I smile up at him. "I'll get these in water right away. And try the soup tomorrow."

"Hope you like it. There's always lots more where that came from."

"I'd love to meet your mother, if that's what you're suggesting."

"I'd love for you to come over. I'll ask. Hey. Do you think the wicked stepsisters are going to give you a hard time for bailing on them?"

I look down at my flowers and scrunch up my nose. Bugger. Our time together was like being frozen inside a magic snow globe. I forgot about the media camped outside of Desie until now, and it completely slipped my mind that I was supposed to meet The Laurens tonight.

"Yes, they are, but I got the Prince, and that's all that matters."

He walks me to the side door and makes sure I can open it. It's already slightly propped open with a small piece of wood, common practice here since many of the girls like to have night visitors and don't want to bother going downstairs to let them in.

"Take away that wood and make sure it's locked, okay?"

I nod, pleased to finally have someone on this continent looking out for me. Once I'm inside, I lean against the open door and watch him walk away.

"Call me tomorrow?" I whisper after him. I don't care if I sound a little desperate. It took me years to find a man like Sam.

"Naw." He turns and smiles. "You'll be busy fielding emails and calls from your adoring fans. I'll write you a letter. It will stand out more." I can't quite tell if he's joking, but I know I'll hear from him again one way or another. I sprint up the stairs two at a time, holding my purple dragon, soup and flowers close to my chest. I can't help but hope I'll get a real letter from Sam. If I did, I'd reread it every night before bed: a beacon of light in this dark modern world.

As I unlock my door and turn on my dresser lamp, I feel my phone vibrate. I place everything on my dresser, then sit on my bed and read the text. It's Sam.

> <Of course, I'll call. But look for a letter, too. Maybe it's a dorky idea, but I think we could get to know one another better that way?>
>
> <I love the idea. Talk tomorrow>

I hit send, then fall back onto my pillow, taking advantage of the near silence in my rarely quiet, nearly dark room to stare up at the ceiling and replay our date in my mind.

The door swings open, the overhead light flares and floods my eyes, and I hear the squeaky voice I've come to loathe. Only, it's booming through the room, and it's squeaky-angry. Bloody hell, it's Barbie with PMS.

"Lauren! Where the fuck were you all night?" Brittany is standing over my bed with Lauren J. by her side. Lauren has her arms folded across her chest, and Brittany is taking a photo of me. I flinch at the bright flash.

"Allow that! I mean, stop that! Did I say you could take a photo of me?" Brittany types something on her phone. Half a second later she looks up, seemingly unfazed that I'm talking directly to her and waiting for an answer.

"I had to tell the other Laurens that we found you. I just posted that in the Facebook group."

"Did you need a photo of me? I'm not a corpse!"

"You were a missing person." Lauren glares at me. "We were expecting you, and you didn't show."

"Missing person? Missing person? I was on a bloody date! Trying to avoid the media you ladies sent my way, no thank you very much." I sit up and kick off my shoes. They land in the corner of the room.

"You went on a date? With Sam? We gave you explicit orders..."

I stand up and face Lauren, who's half a head taller than me. I don't care. She doesn't scare me. In fact, I pity her. All these games she has to play in order to feel in control. "I won't take orders from you. You're not my mum. You're not even a friend. Neither of you are. You were the one who blurted your big ol' hole to the blogger about Sam and me!"

"Where'd you get that silly idea?" Lauren leans back against my desk. "I posted the photo of the Laurens, I admit that, but that was a story I couldn't resist sharing. It was my first big scoop, and I want to be a news anchor someday. So, yes. I tweeted about how we Laurens met, but I didn't give out Sam's last name, or yours. That was someone else."

Brittany steps forward, an inane grin on her face. "It was Sam who spilled everything to the blogger. Then the blogger tipped off all of the reporters, who arrived here, on your doorstep."

I can't believe this. I won't. "That's not true! Sam would never do anything like that!" I just want them out of here. I just want them to leave me alone!

"Think about it." Lauren picks up a nail file on the dresser and starts filing her right pinky nail. "Sam stood to gain the most. Media attention like that could go a long way for someone who wants to gain notoriety at a hospital. We're just the girls he mass-emailed. But Sam is one of the main players in the story. He knew he could be at the center of attention for a long time if he just gave the reporters what they wanted." She pauses and glares into my watery eyes. "So, he did. He gave them you."

"You're full of shite! Get out! You don't live here, get out!"

"Fine, have it your way." She purses her lips and briskly turns for the door. "Brittany, come with. Sleep at my place tonight. She's not stable." She links arms with Brittany, who's still glued to her phone. I wonder how much of this she's going to share online.

"Not stable? My privacy's been invaded, my life turned upside down, and now you're lying about how it happened. Who's the unstable one?"

Lauren shrugs her shoulders and steps out of sight. Brittany turns off the light  before closing the door completely. I'm left standing at the center of the room in total darkness, tears streaming down my cheeks.

It's much too late to call Sam, and besides, what am I supposed to say? I like him so much, and I feel I can trust him. He messed up with how he reached out to me, but everything else about him tells me he's a trustworthy man, a good man.

I fall onto my bed and bury my face into my soft pillow.

I feel more alive than ever when I'm with him, but have I known him long enough to trust him? Damn! These girls are playing with my head!

I open my eyes and hear a loud knock on the door. At first, it's just a tap, but after a few seconds, it sounds progressively more aggressive.

"Brittany. Use your bloomin' key like normal people do!" I shout at the door, then roll over and pull my pillow over my head, but the noise isn't stopping. Persistent bloody cow, that girl.

Begrudgingly, I stumble out of bed as my eyes adjust to the early morning light. I look down to make sure I have pajama pants on. I do.

They're my plaid flannel ones. I groggily remember that after washing my face to try to depuff it from all that crying, I pulled them on along with my fave, oversized T-shirt Lex gave me a few years back. It has the name Gryffindor House in yellow lettering on a red background, and under that, the words Courage, Chivalry, Determination. It always gives me comfort, but at the moment, I wish I were going to school at Hogwarts instead of here. Then at least I could hide under an invisibility cloak from that witch and get some more sleep.

"Brittany, this is the last time I get out of bed when you've forgotten your..." I pull open the door, but I can't finish my sentence. It's not Brittany at our door, not at all. It's the man with big, dark eyes. I remember noticing him staring up at our room yesterday.

Before I have a second to react, he pushes his way into the room and slams the door behind us.

"Hey! I didn't say come in." My voice is hoarse, my breathing unsteady.

"Relax, relax. I'm here to see Brittany. She said drop by anytime." He leans against the closed door and gives me the creepiest smile I've ever seen. He makes Snape look like Santa Claus. I want to vanish. I want my magic cloak!

"Brittany's not here. You should go and come back when she's here." I feel my neck and face growing hot and step backwards toward my phone on my side table. I need to call Sam, this second.

Before I can pick up the phone, he takes a step forward. Then another. I want to tell him to leave, that I'm calling the police, but I've lost my words. I feel like an ice sculpture, frozen in this very spot.

"You're even prettier than Brittany." His eyes grow darker. I didn't think it was possible.

His hands are on my waist. He's pushing me against the desk, grinding his groin against me. I close my eyes for a second, but the adrenaline kicks in, and I open them again, getting a good look at his face.

Don't let this happen. Don't let this happen!

"Stop! Stop!" I'm screaming, but he's got his dry disgusting lips on mine. I'm kicking his shin, kicking his balls, slapping at his face, scratching out his eyes. My bare feet aren't strong enough to do much damage. He takes a stronger grip on me and tries to push me onto the bed. If I don't hurry up and find my strength again, it's all over.

Think, Lauren. Be strong.

I try to calm myself and think back to my self-defense classes. Lexy and I took them together. His breath is hot, he reeks of alcohol; his coarse beard cuts my face. My senses are overloaded. I can only recall that the teacher said she was from Switzerland, and she smelled like she hadn't showered in a week. Lexy made some awful joke about Swiss cheese. What was it she said as we left the last class? Come on, come on, you need to remember. This instant.

"Bend his bloody fingers back. Who woulda thought? Thought it was all about the balls?" We'd laughed at how simple it all sounded and went out for beers to celebrate the last class.

It's all coming back to me. I bend one set of fingers back while pinching him under the armpit. His eyes grow wide with pain. Thank you, sweaty Swiss teacher. Thank you, Lex.

"Fuck!" he mutters.

He releases his grasp on me and bends over in agony. I kick him in the groin again, then race out the door and down the stairwell opposite our room, screaming the entire time.

"Fire! Fire! *Fire!*"

I feel relief wash over my body as I nearly reach the side door entrance, which was left ajar again. Then I trip down the last steps and feel something sharp cut my forehead, my cheek, my eye.

Everything fades to black.

# 16: DELICATE OPERATIONS

## LAUREN

I'm half awake, but my eyelids are so heavy I think it will hurt to open them. The room reeks of bleach and anesthetics. I feel my face throbbing and reach to touch it, but someone is holding my hand. When he squeezes it, the warmth stirs me into the waking world, and I squeeze back.

"Oh my God. Lauren. She's awake, Hank. She's finally awake."

"See Dad, I told you. She's going to be okay."

When I hear Dad's gravelly voice, I open my right eye so I can see him. Bugger. What is wrong with my other eye? It feels like it's glued shut.

"Did they catch him?" I sound like a little kid with laryngitis. I look at Dad with my one good eye and start to sit up. My big brother steps forward and gently presses my left shoulder so I'm lying back down.

"Lauren, you need to rest," he says. "You've been asleep for two whole days. You were badly hurt."

"No kidding! I thought I just had the bloody stomach flu," I snark at Hank, using that little sister tone he's come to expect from me, then try to smile a little. I'm quite certain it's coming out lopsided. It must be the painkillers. They aren't working very well. I feel like I was hit by a train in the face, and then it backed up and drove over me one more time. I'm also bloody uncomfortable in this tight-fitting olive-green nightshirt. I don't know whose it is, but it doesn't suit me one little bit, and it feels itchy against my skin.

"Tell me they caught the slimebucket who attacked me!"

"I'm sorry, Lauren. Not yet." Dad hands me a glass of water with a straw in it. I put it back down at my bedside table.

A nurse who's been buzzing around the bed for five minutes now wraps a blood pressure cuff around my arm and says, "Hushhh."

I want to tell her this is possibly *the* worst time to take my blood pressure, but she's just told me to hush, and I do try to obey authorities. When she's finished, she takes the cuff off, picks up a tablet off my side table, taps a couple times on it, then nods at me to continue my conversation.

"The police are working on it," Hank tells me. "So far they've only had help from the residence don who brought you into emerg. They need your statement."

"Michael brought me in? Of course, he did. Only one I liked on my entire floor." I rest my head back into the pillow, trying to get comfortable as a flood of memories rush through me. I don't want to remember any of it, but I can't help it. As tears well in my eyes, Hank sees the pained expression on my face and puts his arms around me.

"I can help you speak with the authorities," Hank says. "I'll stay a while and help you through everything." I nod, not the least bit surprised that Hank is the one stepping up emotionally. Dad's here, at least. That's a start. I have to take his being here as a step in the right direction. Never would have expected Natalie; she's still breastfeeding Zachary with a two-year-old tugging at her pantleg. But where's Mum?

"He didn't do anything to me," I say, realizing they probably don't know. "Scuffed me up a little, that's all." I pull the covers up to my chest. "Is Mum on her way?"

"She just called from Cannes, sweetie," Hank says. "She's speaking at a medical conference and can't get away. But she's said she's going to Facetime you the minute you wake up..."

"Yet, somehow you managed to come from even farther than Cannes." I swallow the hard lump in my throat and try not to cry. My bandaged eye and the bridge of my nose are hot and tender, and my dry mouth tastes like stale peppermints. I could use a hug from Mum right about now, and yet, I don't want to speak with her ever again.

"Your mother spoke with the doctor, and he reassured her that all your vitals were good. We knew you were just resting." Dad leans over to stroke my hair and tucks a strand behind my ear for me. Maybe it's the pain in my left eye or this lumpy bed, but I want to swat his hand away. My own mother can't make it to see me in the hospital? Did she send Dad? Is it his turn to deal with me? Do they pass me off like a football?

Hank sees my expression and speaks again. "Lexy's just texted. She's got two papers to finish, but she's looking into flights."

My breathing steadies and my heart swells with warmth and faith again. You can't choose your family, but you can choose your friends.

"Laur..." Dad's not a stupid man. He knows I'm peeved. I can't even make eye contact with him. "Lauren. I think your mother is avoiding me. We haven't been in the same room in a long while..."

"You don't think exactly now, exactly this moment, is the time for you two to set aside your differences? Come together for your hurt little girl?" I shout. I feel my face and chest flushing with rage.

"Listen up. We're doctors. We went over your file. We knew you were going to be okay!" He runs his hand through his wavy salt and pepper hair and clears his throat. He always does that when he's anxious.

"Oh, so I'm your patient, am I? Don't let emotion cloud your judgment? That certainly worked all my life. I'm so bloody sick of you two and that British stiff upper lip you feel obliged to wear! Maybe I needed you to wrap your arms around me once in a while, not just offer me a bandage. Why do you think I really ran away to Canada? To get away from you two!"

Dad flinches and turns to face the window as I shout the last part. At the same time, a tall, achingly good-looking doctor steps into the room. He gives us an awkward look and starts to turn to leave.

"No, Dr. Marshal, please, come in," Hank says. "Lauren, this is the doctor who performed your surgery. You had a laceration to your left eye, right at the bridge of your nose, but he stitched you up real good."

"Hi, Lauren." Dr. Marshal steps forward and grins at me, and I feel my heart flutter in its chest cavity. He's not only soap-opera gorgeous, but his deep voice belongs on the radio. "You slept a lot after your anesthetic, and we're giving you morphine and intravenous fluids to help you out. You probably feel groggy, and you might start feeling angry or even fearful because you were attacked. I want to keep monitoring your eye another day or so before we release you, and I'll recommend a therapist who specializes in talking about this kind of incident."

"This kind of incident? You mean rape? I can say it, doctor. I'm fine. He didn't rape me." As I say the words, I realize I'm shaking under the covers.

"Yes, but he tried to. Lauren, I think it's wise you speak to someone."

"I just want to go home. When can I go home?" I clench my fists into a ball on my lap and swallow hard.

"You can come home to live with me and Denise as soon as they release you, sweetheart," Dad answers.

"Dad... you really think that's wise?" Hank is glaring at him. "She doesn't get along with Denise. She was enjoying life at TFU, for the most part."

"That's bare jokes, were you even reading my texts?" I shout at him. "I met someone wonderful, but it ended up all over the internet. Some amoeba-brained bitches took over, and I was harassed by them, then attacked by a madman who I can only assume was an escape convict from a nearby penitentiary!"

"So, I don't care if I have to live with the stupid cow who stole my dad from my mum. I want to leave this town and never come back!"

As I shout those final words, I lose all my breath and need to lower my head between my knees to avoid hyperventilating. Hank rubs my back and tells me to take long, deep breaths. When I look up a second later, I nearly lose my breath all over again.

Sam is standing in the doorway.

# 17: THE EYE OF THE STORM

**SAM**

"Jake... Dr. Marshal, can I... I know the patient... would it be ok..." I look at my Resident in Chief, and as soon as he gives me a silent nod, I rush to Lauren's bedside, bend down to her level and wrap my arms around her.

"You had me worried. I'm so glad you're awake. You're going to be okay." She looks at me with tears glistening in her eyes, and I lean in and kiss her gently on the lips. It seemed like the right thing to do when I saw her looking at me like that, but she pulls away from my embrace. She's not even looking at me anymore. Her head is turned, and she's looking out the window.

"I'm sorry I wasn't there," I mutter. "I'd have killed him. If I'd been there..."

"But you weren't there, were you son," the man I assume to be Lauren's father interjects. "You sent the paparazzi her way. You're to blame for this. All of this." He walks up to me, so close I can feel his hot breath on my collarbone. I take a step back.

"Sir, with all due respect, we don't know if the attacker was a member of the media, or just a criminal who came in through the side door."

"Dad," Lauren speaks up. "Sam's right. That door shouldn't have been propped open like that. I always thought so."

"Still," her father's face is as red as a tomato. "You shouldn't be here. I want you to leave."

"Dr. Green, this is a teaching hospital. Sam's doing rotations, and he's here to learn. Would you mind if he just stays to talk to me about Lauren's treatment?" Jake asks.

"Fine, fine, just stay away from my daughter." He turns abruptly so his back is facing me and walks back to Lauren's bedside. I expect her to interrupt him and tell him he's wrong, to defend me and let him know how she feels about me. She does none of these things. She's still staring out the window.

Jake takes me by the elbow and pulls me over to the wall by the door. I keep my eyes on Lauren, hoping that she'll look at me, too. She isn't budging. Is it because of the torment that she's been through, or is she angry with me for some unknown reason that I may never know because I'm a guy who's not getting it? Because that's the vibe that I'm getting from her, and it's more than unsettling.

However, I'm at work, and I have a job to do. I have to try to shake this off for a few minutes.

"How do we go about stitching up a bridge laceration like the one I sutured in this patient?" Jake asks me, and the growing group of interns behind me. He must have texted them to join our impromptu class. I look behind me and see Ronny whispering to Lucy and Stephen, who glance over at me. They're probably talking about who Lauren is and exchanging details about the whole mass-emailing fiasco. Now this. Will this go viral too? *Buen Dios* please don't let this get out online. Lauren deserves some privacy. She needs it more than ever after what she's just gone through.

"Children." Jake turns and scolds the group behind me. "Shut your mouths and listen for once. This is a prime example of the kind of injury you'll see in emerg when you're working residents. That's coming up sooner than you think. Do you want to know what you're doing so you can repair somebody's face, or do you only want to know the idle gossip you're sharing?"

Lucy's face flushes, as does Ronny's neck. They lower their heads.

I raise my left hand at waist-level to get Jake's attention. He nods, so I continue. "I'd say the first step is to suspect a lacrimal duct injury, based on remembering the relevant anatomy. You probably consulted with an

116

ophthalmologist for this surgery? It's vital to ensure Lauren doesn't end up with a serious problem in coming weeks."

"Good, Sam. I'm impressed." Jake doesn't smile and keeps looking at his tablet, but the words are what I needed to hear. I need Lauren to know I'm looking out for her. She's finally looking over at me with that one good eye; the other is bandaged with a clear plastic tegaderm shield that blocks the eye but allows her medical team exposure to the wound.

There it is. We're fine. She needs me, just as much as I need her.

Wait. No. I'm wrong. She isn't looking at me at all. She's looking at Jake.

"As a general principle," Jake continues, walking over to Lauren and placing his hand on her shoulder, "always consult with a surgeon who specializes in the anatomy of what you're trying to fix. Consider what lies beneath the skin surface. This technique will help you to avoid missing important vascular and tendon injuries too. Any questions?"

"Did she have a duct injury?" I ask, not looking at him directly.

"No, she didn't, but she had a laceration close to it, so we used a stent. It was serious, but she'll be fine in a matter of weeks. She'll have to visit our out-patient clinic once a week for a month, okay Lauren? You live close enough?"

"I don't think I'm staying in Edwin Cove after all of... this... but thanks for all that you did." She looks up at him and smiles a smile I felt had been reserved for me alone. I want to give Jake a laceration or two.

Jake swats his hand at the interns, and they disperse like flies. He takes Lauren's hand.

"Sam? I know you're on my duty today, but could you leave me for a minute to speak with my patient and her family?"

Lauren isn't even looking at me. She's still studying Jake's face. Her father and Hank are in the far corner of the room having a private conversation. I turn and leave the room.

Jake? She's smitten with Jake? I've heard of the Nightingale effect, but this is ridiculous. This would be the effect in reverse. Besides, I doubt he'll ever develop real feelings for Lauren. He's a player, and from the locker room stories I've heard, not a good person in the end. This has to be just temporary. She'll come back around. She has to.

A nagging thought decides to rent space in my brain, and it won't vacate the premises: *I've been wrong about women and their feelings for me before, but this is the first time it matters.*

# 18: CALL ME DR. JAKE

## LAUREN

Dr. Marshal fluffed both my pillows for me and asked the nurse to get my lunch tray. Doctor. Jake. Marshal... even his name is like buttered popcorn melting on my tongue. He's like one of those soap-opera doctors who's also a fitness model in his spare time.

I'm wondering if the painkillers are now in fact working, because I'm loopier than usual. I can't stop thinking silly girly thoughts, like how the doctor's firm biceps flexed and brushed my neck when he bent over me to inspect my eye, and how very close his face was to mine. He told me he'd take care of me until I was completely healed, and for a moment it felt like I was his only patient in the entire hospital, and maybe a little more.

He is delicious, and I'm delusional. I'm looking for something to distract me from the dilemma that is Sam. I know I have to speak to him alone, to find out if what the Laurens said is true, but Dad banished him from my room—possibly my life—and I didn't do a thing to stop him.

Well, why should I? If he's been lying to me...

Could the Laurens be right? Has he been playing me this entire time to get media attention, maybe even money for his interviews? It's expensive going to med school. Could that be what's going on? I can't forgive him if that's true.

Dr. Marshal, Dad and Hank are in deep discussion by the window. The sill is lined with four potted orange and yellow begonias and four sparkly cards with butterflies, rainbows and the words GET WELL in bubble letters. I've hit the bloody jackpot. All this, and a busted-up eye!

119

More than I ever get at Christmas! I want to laugh and cry at once. So that's it, then. I've been had this entire time. What do I even fecking know about university life? I only did a year in the UK, and I hardly attended classes or social events because of what I was going through at home and with Lexy. There are far more of them than there are of me, and I allowed a disgusting thug in my room, so what do I even know? Buggernuts. What if Lauren J. is telling the truth?

I can't cry, simply must not cry; I'll get this bandage wet and then my eye might fall out of its socket, and I have no bloody idea if we have proper insurance for any of this nonsense. As I try to steady my breathing, I look up to see Dr. Marshal standing over me.

"Dr. Marshal... I want to go home with my dad..." I sniffle between the tears that come anyway. My phone in my jacket pocket on the chair in the corner pings a notification, then a second, and a third. Not this. Please, no. I can't be Twitterverse trending all over again.

"I don't think that's the right thing to do, Lauren, you need to be cared for here. And if that sound means what I think it means, I don't think you should check your phone for a while. Maybe take down your accounts and get a new number." Dr. Marshal says. Hank finds the phone in my jacket, turns off the ringer and puts the disturbance away in his own pocket.

"I'm fine. I'll be fine! But I can't live in that... that place... where it all happened!" I turn to look at Hank. He reaches over and puts his hands on my shoulders, so we're eye to eye.

"Wren, you don't have to. We'll move you somewhere else. Okay? Dr. Marshal here has an idea. Dr., go ahead and tell her." Hank hands me the ice water at my bedside. I look at it and put it back down again. They should know by now I bloody hate drinks with ice in them. If I could have my beer here served warm, I would. Bloody hate the cold. What the hell am I even doing here in Canada?

"A doctor I work with here and his wife are looking for a roommate. One of those attic bedrooms, real nice. They aren't having a family yet, so they want to rent out the extra room for the time being. It would be perfect. They're a stable couple; great people. It's on Layton, close to campus, but not a long walk to the hospital, either. He could drive you here for your appointments sometimes, too.

"I glace at Hank, who looks at Dad for guidance. Dad shrugs his shoulders. I'm not sure what I even want to do, but I know Hank always has my back.

"Dr. Marshal, could I have a minute with my brother and father?" I ask. He gives me a quick but discernible wink. A wink! I wasn't imagining it.

"You bet. And, Dr. Marshal is my Grandpa. Call me Dr. Jake." He leaves us, closing the door behind him.

"Did you mean it when you said you hate living here?" Hank takes my hand.

"No, no of course not." I look down at my lap. "I'm just angry that this happened to me and... I guess I wanted to run again."

"Run?"

"Yeah, when things didn't work out with Alex... and Mum and Dad split and weren't even talking to me..." I let my voice trail off and find the courage to look up. The expression on Dad's face is one I've never seen before. He looks angry, and I realize after studying his eyes that he's angry at himself.

"I thought you left to have an adventure..."

"That too, Dad, that too. But you really fucked things up with Mum... and with me..."

He runs his fingers through his hair and clears his throat, takes a step forward and takes my other hand.

"I fucked it up. I did. And I'm sorry." He gives my hand a squeeze.

I close my eyes. Everyone's quiet for a second, until Hank bursts out in bellowing laughter.

"Dad just admitted wrongdoing. I need to call Mum."

# 19: MOVING DAY

**One week later**

## LAUREN

"I thought Canadians were always nice." Hank calls from the oak stairwell behind me.

I open my bedroom door and walk inside the bright, white room. It smells clean, like lemon Lysol wipes, but it's too medicinal and overpowering for my liking. I make a mental note to burn an apple spice candle the second I'm alone in my new surroundings.

"That's an overused stereotype, but I'd have to say that they are, for the most part."

"Well then it would have been nice for Jake to warn us about the stairs. The. Endless. Flights. Of..." Hank takes a breath before taking the last step up to my new bedroom. "Stairs."

I take the heavy box from him and move aside to let him through the door. He collapses dramatically on the grey sofa under the skylight window and sprawls his long legs out, arms dangling to the floor.

"Oh, give it a rest brother, you work in construction. You should have endless endurance!" I shove the box up against the wall with the others. It was a relief to have Dad and Hank offer to empty out my room at Desie so I didn't have to deal with the memories or speak to Brittany or one single Lauren. When he heard the move was going to happen, Sam loaned us his truck, but he and Jake both had shifts at the hospital, so Hank's been at the wheel. It would have been awkward having both Sam and Jake help out, especially with Dad being so surly towards Sam at the

123

hospital. I was relieved when he let Sam offer over his truck keys without an argument. I'm sure Hank convinced Dad to ease off a little.

"I'm more management these days. Tripp is gallivanting the world with his wife every other bloody month," Hank says.

I walk to the corner bar and sink and grab a white coffee mug hanging over the small marble counter. Dr. Pandya, the homeowner, remodeled this old attic bedroom last summer so it would work like a bachelor apartment. It has its own separate entrance with two secure doors. The bathroom is across the hall, but I'm the only one using it, and there's another door in that hallway leading downstairs to the family kitchen. My bathroom has one of those deep soaker tubs with claw feet! I loved the space the second I set eyes on it and knew it was where I needed to be.

I pour Hank the rest of the coffee left in the small pot and hand him the mug. "After a brief rest, do you think you can manage the last few boxes, or are you going to leave our poor father standing alone beside Sam's truck?"

"I think we should leave him groveling a little longer. Besides, he's having a good chat with Dr. Pandya."

When Hank grins, his face lights up the whole room. He's basically a male Julia Roberts. I forgot how much I missed hanging out with him. He sits up and puts the hot coffee on the small glass table in front of him.

Sitting on the right corner of my new queen bed, I curl my feet in so they're touching and adjust my plastic eye patch. It's irritating my skin, and though I can see through it, it has me walking off-kilter, but Jake says it can't be removed until bedtime. I wiggle my toes, trying to feel them again. It's grown rather chilly here this week. My thick red socks stand out against the fresh white quilt. I don't know why, but it makes me think of the sock Christmas stockings Mum gave us, and all the good times we had before our family broke apart.

"A little groveling doesn't go a long way. Not with me. You should know that."

"You have always held your grudges tight to your chest. Just like that *Star Wars* Lego set you'd never let me touch." He takes a sip of coffee and pouts dramatically.

"The Ewok village? Bloody right I wouldn't let you touch it. I spent three days making that thing, and you had Princess Leia attack the Ewoks and posted the video to YouTube!"

"You were seven. This has seriously scarred you for life?" Hank can't hide his delight.

"It was more that you involved my poor innocent cat Princess Leia in the destruction!" I bite my lower lip to try to hide the chuckles I feel coming on.

"Innocent my arse. That cat roamed around at night collecting the neighbor's socks and undies. Ma still has someone's ghastly grape Fruit of the Looms hanging on her Wall of Shame in the guest room."

"Bugger, that Wall of Shame was creepy. How could Leia have possibly dragged in that orange velour bathrobe from outside? It obviously came from nineteen fifty-five!"

"And yet, there it hung, for years. We'll never know why."

"Maybe Mum was losing it even back then."

"You think she's losing it now?" Hank laughs.

"It's the only explanation for not visiting me in the hospital."

Hank gets up and walks right over to me. "Lauren. She is avoiding Dad. That is all." He says it sternly, like this is the last time we'll speak of it. He reaches out one hand to help pull me up.

"I just wish we were all together again. It was so good then." I choke back tears. He pulls me in for a tight squeeze.

"I know, Wren, I remember. Sometimes the past is best left in the past. It's painful to look behind us when now is all we can truly control. At least Dad is here with us. Maybe I can bring Béa and the baby back for Christmas. Would you like that?"

I sniffle into his shirt. I hope I didn't muck it up. "I'd love to meet Reece before his first birthday, but why wouldn't I go back home?"

He pulls pack and looks at me intently. It's that stern look again. "Because you need to be here for the therapy, Lauren. It's important you make those sessions for... for a long while."

"The first session didn't do a bloody thing." I sigh. "I mean, I liked the therapist. She was nice and all. But I still want to rip my attacker's throat out with my teeth."

"You do, do you? The first day in hospital you said you were just fine. I would say you're making progress."

I laugh and punch him on his upper arm like I've done since I was five. It always hurts me more than it hurts him. "Point made, bring the family for Christmas, but I won't be cooking. I don't have much of a kitchen." I head for the door.

"No, no, don't cook." Hank follows me down the stairs. "We've had enough recent tragedies. We don't need food poisoning to ruin our holiday."

I turn on the stairs, laughing. "You're cheeky and condescending in your old age, aren't you? Does your wife put up with this?"

"It's all part of the therapy, Patch. *Argh, matey*, watch yourself on the stairs."

"Stop calling me Patch!" I yell over my shoulder, knowing it's no use. I jump off the last step onto the sunny sidewalk, smiling to myself as I see Dad laughing with Dr. Pandya. Dad in his vintage grey Stetson hat throwing his head back in one direction; Dr. Pandya in his royal blue turban nodding in laughter in the same direction. A bright red leaf dances over their heads; two pirouettes later it gets caught in a late October wind gust and soars up the gabled rooftops. I want to snap a photo for Lex, who always appreciates art.

I zip up my leather jacket, tuck my hands in my pockets, and lift my face toward the sun. I'm going to be okay, in the end. I have a long way to go before I've healed inside and out, but I have loyal friends and family to turn to.

I only wish I knew... can I still count Sam as one of those friends?

It looks like someone painted the sky up there, just for me. I stretch my legs out across the sofa and hang my head back over the arm rest to stare up at my magnificent skylight view. The sky is a clear, crisp Mediterranean blue. It looks more like August than October. A crow or a blackbird—I don't know my birds—soars overhead. I'm mesmerized, and for the first time in over a week, I feel serene. I hope Dad and Hank take longer than promised to pick up the Thai food—our makeshift Thanksgiving dinner, as we just realized it's Thanksgiving here in Canada, and I had one sad and empty fridge.

There's a knock at the door. I sit upright fast, clench my fists. Just as my heart starts to race, I remember where I am. I'm safe here, with good people. I don't need to be afraid of a little tap on the door. Still, I walk to it with trepidation and leave the gold latch chain on the door.

"Who is it?"

"Lauren, it's me. Please, can we talk?"

The second I hear Sam's voice, my heart races again. "I thought you needed to be at the hospital?" I say through the door. I've missed him: how he makes me laugh, how he lets me be myself. But I needed the week to sort out what I was feeling. I probably should have at least answered his texts.

"I was, but I left for a bit. One of my buddies said he'd cover me for an hour. Saif... I mean Dr. Pandya... he just let me in the outside door."

Sam seems to already have lots of respect from his fellow colleagues, so why would he even have motivation to do what the Laurens said he did? I searched for any online proof that he'd been the one to tip off the reporters about our story, and I couldn't find anything, but the blogger did refer to the hashtag #laurenfromlastnight, which I noticed Lauren J.

first coined. Still, just logging onto Twitter and seeing I now have 45K followers made me feel sick to my stomach. All of this attention, all because Sam wanted me! It was flattering at first, but it has grown into something Sam never intended, something I can't manage.

Hank erased all of my social media accounts yesterday, and Dad bought me a new phone. I just want to pretend none of this ever happened. I need to get back to classes tomorrow and start fresh. The court case for that filthy stalker sleaze? I don't even want to think about having to testify. I hope he pleads guilty so that I don't have to. I'm not sure I can survive that process. I read that four out of five sexual assault cases in Canada never make it to court, and for the ones that do make it to court, only a little over half result in convictions.

Physical assault cases like mine must not make it to trial nearly as often. I'm sure most young women don't bother forcing the issue because many of them feel they won't be believed. My therapist and I discussed my chances, and it did lift a weight off my shoulders. Police grabbed his DNA from my fingernails, and it matches two unsolved rape cases. I feel lucky to have gotten out of that room with just a busted-up eye and broken spirit. I want this horrible excuse of a human being to serve time for what he did to me and those other women, and I need to know he won't be able to harm anyone again. Either way, Hank promises he'll be by my side. Jake has promised to be there, too.

So where does all of this leave Sam? I unlock the chain and open the door to find out.

# 20. COMPARING ASTERS AND ROSES

## LAUREN

"I picked these purple asters from the garden. Can't believe they're still growing, even with the leaves falling and covering them. Persistent buggers. Makes me think of you—your strength." Sam's voice cracks slightly as he hands me a delicate purple bouquet tied with an orange satin ribbon and a white envelope. He remains standing on the top step, one foot still on the step below, as if waiting on the invisible threshold between yesterday and tomorrow. As always, he looks strong and solid to the core despite the uncertainty he must be feeling.

"I also wrote you this letter," he says. "It may border on cheesy. I dunno... it was my father's idea, and since Ma and him have lasted longer than most. I just thought..." His voice trails off as he looks down at his feet. He clears his throat and sighs.

"Once again, I'm standing here feeling like these gestures are not enough, considering what you've gone through..."

He looks up at me. There's that sexy, under-stated sideways smile lighting up my life again. *I'm supposed to be angry at you, stop that, Sam.*

"So, I thought I'd invite you to my family's for dinner. It's Thanksgiving Day here, not sure you would know that just getting out of hospital... and..." He sounds breathless.

"Thanks Sam, they're lovely." I take a whiff of the bouquet. There are sprigs of Heather and a hint of chocolate mint in the bouquet, and I want to ask him who puts all the work into this magical garden. I suspect he does a lot of it. He seems to have that kind of attention to detail, and I think it will serve him well as a surgeon.

129

"Come in, come in. We actually have plans for supper, Dad's getting take-away...Thai, on Princess?" I motion for him to have a seat on the sofa and put the letter on the side table and the flowers in the empty blue pitcher on the coffee table. I'll have to add water later.

As I glance at him, I see him looking around the room, and his eyes rest on the small corner bar area where I left the twenty-four red roses Jake sent over. They're in a tall glass vase, and there are so many they overwhelm the counter area. The card that sits against the vase says *XO-J.* and can be read from where we're sitting. Sam sees me looking at him and quickly moves his eyes away from the roses back to his lap.

"But it was a nice thought... thank your parents... and your flowers are so pretty... really," I say. Now there's an awkward storm cloud hanging above us, and I just want it to be gone.

"Did have some mashed potatoes and gravy in the hospital. I think they were from a package," I add. "Tasted like cardboard and sewer sludge. Mingin'"

"That's gross." He's wringing his hands in his lap. "I know that Thai place. It's good."

"Great."

"Lauren... Are you feeling okay? Did you... is the talking with that therapist helping?"

"Talking about it helps a little, I guess. I just want to see him locked up."

"Yeah, me too. If I can help at all—anything—I'm always here."

"Thanks." I could kiss him. I want to, but I resist. I quickly stand and look out the window behind the sofa.

I don't know how to ask him. I don't know if I should. Sitting here beside him feels right, and it feels easy, but it's been so complicated with Sam. We always seem to be running from something. A flooded bar, the relentless media. I wish it could be easy for us.

"Sam, did you share our story? About how you went looking for me and mass-emailed? Did you talk to reporters about that?" The second it spills out of my lips, I regret it.

"What? How could you even think..." Sam stands. He's turned pale.

"Lauren J. says it was you. That she didn't speak to any reporters, but word is you did."

"And you trust those Laurentuplets over me?" he shouts. "They created the hashtag and tried to hold you hostage from me!" I've never heard Sam raise his voice before. I suppose it's warranted; I'm just not used to hearing it. There's a lot of hurt in his voice.

"No, I guess not... Sam! I don't bloody know what to think anymore!" I can't help but raise my voice in return. My eyes sting with tears; my stitches feel like hot coals on my skin.

"Shhh." Sam walks up to me, wraps his arm around my waist and wipes the tears from my left cheek. "I didn't mean to upset you. Please don't cry. I just can't believe you'd think I would do something like that. I really like you. I have your back more than anyone here. I thought you knew that."

"Sam..." I bury my whole face into his chest, so I don't have to look at him. I'd forgotten how wonderful he smells, like coming home to spiced candles and mulled wine simmering on the stove.

"I don't think we should see each other anymore," I blurt. "The press, all the online attention, it will finally go away if we aren't together. I can't take everyone still talking about us! It's just all too complicated."

"There's got to be another way..." He gently lifts my chin to look at him, but I pull it down and pull out of his arms.

"Can you just leave? I'm tired, and my family will be back soon."

He stares at me, his hazel eyes sadder than I've ever seen them before. Possibly sadder than when he told me about his sister's death. Our long silence feels like that eerie calm before a thunderstorm sweeps in. What have I done?

"So, we have to break up because of what other people think? I thought you, of all people, didn't give a bloody buggernuts fuck about what other people thought."

I blink and take a step toward him. I didn't know he could talk like that.

"Sam—"

"I guess I was wrong." He turns on his heels, and I think he might even slam the door, but he stops in the doorway. "I'll miss you. Get your new boyfriend to look at your stitches. They might be infected."

Before I can say anything back, he's gone.

# 21. MY HEART IS WILD HAGGIS

## Lauren's Diary—KEEP OUT!

*Oh, it's you again. Never bloody mind, come have a sit under my new skylight and a glass of cheap wine Dad bought me as a room-warming gift because he was feeling guilty for... well, absolutely everything, I'd say. And so he should. At least he showed up.*

*I read somewhere that showing up is eighty percent of what makes a successful life. If you can show up, you'll be successful at life, because most mornings you just want to pull up the covers and stay in bed.*

*Show up. Can't say that much for Mum. She does, however, show up to all of her blasted medical conferences. A plus for that.*

*Sorry I can't offer anything stronger to drink—new room and all. Still unpacking.*

*Yes, it's after five. It's bloody three o'dark in the morning, but I can't sleep. I've just done something that may have been the biggest mistake of my life. I pushed Sam away. Why did I do that? Why do I do any of the things I do?*

*Poor Sam. He was only trying to make me feel special. When I was with him, I never felt like hashtag news, the viral story of the fall. That's how everyone else around here has made me feel. But he made me feel unique and precious, like a snowflake. He also caught the mistake on how my eye was stitched up, which would have caused a massive infection. And I treated him* like snow-plow leftovers: that dirty brown mush on the side of the street.

The worst part is I think I love him. But he's just not good for me. Is he?

Why do I even keep a bloody diary? They're always about things that happened in the past. Things I can't control anymore. Like falling in love. Nobody chooses who they love. It just happens.

I didn't choose to fall for Sam, end up the viral story of the fall, and get both our hearts mangled into meat pie in the process. Or haggis. My heart is wild haggis. Stop looking at me like that. Go on, have some more wine, then. I'll fill you in on the beautiful madness of a mess that is my life.

# 22. ANSWERED PRAYERS

## LAUREN

*CLANG! CLANG! TING.*

I can hear Mrs. Pandya—*Farida*. She's already told me a few times to call her Farida, which she says means "unique"—messing about in the kitchen downstairs. Pots have been clanging and glasses clinking together for five minutes now, along with beautiful singing in a language foreign to me. The combination of metal, glass and female vocals is surprisingly melodic. Farida is either emptying the dishwasher or performing some kind of morning Indian ritual. I hope it's the former, because the area around my left eye and the bridge of my nose are so itchy and inflamed, I'm not going to be much help with the latter. My rhythm is off on a good day; with my eye in this state, I'll be lucky if I make it from these stairs to the kitchen table without knocking something important over.

"Oh, my dear! That eye! Not good. Not good at all." Farida sees me walking slowly towards her, puts down the glass in her hand, takes me by the elbow and leads me to a chair. She was wearing a flowing red and gold saree the day that I met her, but now she's in dark jeans and a lovely orange blouse that contrasts with her raven locks. She looks like a runway model, and it's only seven in the morning.

"I once had a cat that used to drag things into the house. I'm literally something the bloody cat dragged in." I say, looking down at my loose, long-sleeved white t-shirt and baggy jogging pants.

"Does it hurt?" She bends down to look into my left eye. I took the plastic shield off last night. Maybe I shouldn't have because that's when it started to swell. Okay, I did some serious pillow-crying late last night after Dad and Hank caught their flight home. I'm sure the tears didn't help matters.

"A little. I'm going to walk to ECGH to get Jake to take a look at the stitches," I explain.

"Oh, my goodness! Your eye looks like a mandrill's butt cheek." Dr. Pandya is standing in the doorway in his royal blue scrubs and matching turban, car keys and cell phone in his right hand. I laugh out loud at his comment, but when I see Farida frowning at him, I decide to stop.

"Saif!" She scolds her husband. "Be nice. Her family just left, poor girl."

"I'm being nice, and I'm being realistic. Lauren needs antibiotics. I'll drive."

"That would be great, thanks so much," I say, getting up from the table.

"You don't want to eat anything first?" She motions to the counter, which is covered in flour leftover from whatever she's been baking this morning. I whiff the air. It's permeated with cumin and carrots and several spices I can't place. What's in that green sauce on the table?

"You know I never turn down your samosas. We'll take them in the car." Dr. Pandya puts his phone in his pocket and snaps up two triangular shaped pastries off the plate on the kitchen table, then starts to shake his hands, a surprised look on his face. He drops them back on the plate.

"They're still hot, Saif! How do you not know this by now?" Farida rolls her eyes, grabs two different samosas and puts them in a brown bag for us. "You want to burn those surgeon fingers? Do we need to insure them as well as the house?"

Dr. Pandya laughs and kisses her firmly on the cheek. "No. No, you'll take care of me. You are too good to me." Farida blushes like a newlywed at his kiss, rearranges her orange blouse on her shoulders and waves her husband away, her gold wrist bangles jingling as she does so.

"Go, go save lives."

"Bye," I say and follow Dr. Pandya out of the kitchen, into the hallway, past the small dark room to the right. He gives me the "one sec" sign, so I stand in the hallway as he ducks inside the room to grab a blue encyclopedia on the ottoman. There's a brown and gold prayer mat on the floor and an ornate gold lamp on the coffee table, along with a pitcher and comb.

Dr. Pandya stops in the doorway, catching me staring at the items. I feel my face flushing. It's possibly redder than my swollen eye.

"Are you religious Lauren?"

"Not really," I shake my head and look at the prayer mat again. "I believe in something. Angels more than anything, I think?"

"Why is that?"

"Something led our residence don to find me lying on the bottom step that night, before it was too late." I feel silly talking about this, but his gentle smile instantly puts me at ease.

"Yes. Personal beliefs are important for growth," he says. "Never conform to another's beliefs. You've got to cultivate your own garden." He glances back to the room once more, and I sense that, for him, this space is the garden he's speaking about.

"The steps I take in prayer," he says, motioning to the rug and pitcher, "they're so much like the steps I take before a surgery. I've always been Muslim, but as I've grown closer to Allah, I've become a more skilled surgeon. Present in prayer, present in surgery."

I nod and study the room once more, then follow him out the front door. It's cold and pouring rain out, so we dash to the car. As Dr. Pandya gets in and I buckle up in the passenger seat, he brushes raindrops off his coat, then hands me a samosa.

"I've never had one of these," I say, biting into what tastes like warm pie crust and soft potato filling. I can't believe what I'm tasting. I can never eat enough of these for the rest of my living days.

"Ah, ah see?" Dr. Pandya grins as my eyes widen, and my eyebrows raise higher and higher in delight.

"Mmmph!" is all I can muster. Eyes closed, I'm savoring every morsel. My taste buds are overwhelmed.

"That is Paradise rolled into a pastry," he says as he pulls the car into the street. "Now, let's get that infection healed. Don't worry, it probably just needs ointment. I'll drive you home after."

A group of about fifteen preschoolers in yellow, red and blue rain slickers and boots are waddling single file along the wet, leaf-covered sidewalk. Their brightly colored mittens cling to a yellow rope like it's their mothers' hands. As our car passes by, a few let go to point and wave at us.

My eyes water, but I don't think it's the samosa spices. It's a bittersweet longing for a home in England that really isn't home anymore. It's also gratitude. I'm grateful I was forced to let go of my rope and relieved that I decided to stay.

"Does this hurt?" Dr. Jake is holding up a small flashlight while peering into my left eye. As he holds the light, his left bicep bulges like a baseball under his blue scrubs sleeve. His amber eyes are about half an inch from mine, so close I can see the yellow flecks in them. His breathing is shallow and steady, and it warms my lips and neck.

*No, it doesn't hurt, Jake,* I want to say, *actually, quite the opposite. Please don't check my heart rate right now. Please, can we not go there?*

"My eyes don't hurt on the inside. Just the bridge of the nose and under the eye where it's swollen. There's a little bit of pus in the corner, though." I try to say this evenly, but it comes out like a series of squeaks.

"Alright." He backs away and keeps staring at me. I look down at the examination table, lean back and accidentally scrunch the sheet of tissue paper with my hands. When I sit back up again, it rips once more. It sounds like we're in a shoe store and can't make up our minds. I cross my arms over my chest, trying to keep them out of trouble.

"Lauren, you've got an infection beneath one of your stitches where your eye meets your nose. I'm glad I caught it."

He caught it? I decide not to correct him. He's my doctor; I'm supposed to be listening to his instructions, not thinking about 3D mini-golf and kisses in the dark.

"I'll have one of my interns pull out the old stitch, clean and re-stitch it. You'd be in better hands with me doing it," Jake grins and his teeth take up half his face, "but I have a major surgery." He lowers his voice a little. "Still picking you up for dinner tonight, though, right?"

"Yes, sure, although, you may have to carry me to the table."

"I'd carry you into the sunset, sweetheart," Jake says this with a southern drawl and grins again, but I can't decipher if he's purposefully being cheesy or not. I attempt a sideways smile but suddenly feel like a criminal sitting here talking with my doctor about our date. I don't think it's a crime to date your doctor-who-wasn't-really-your-doctor-anymore-until-you-got-an-infection, but I'm a foreigner and inexperienced at life, what do I know? I should be asking Lexy about this. She knows the ins and outs of every social trend and meme before it fails to impress anyone anymore and becomes what she calls a "dead meme." I wish she'd answer her damn phone for once. She did text yesterday to see how I was doing in the new place, and to say that she's losing sleep over her final term essays. I got excused from most of mine, so I can't complain.

Of course, I'll have to tell her he didn't really take no for an answer about dinner. That's sexy, right? A man who knows what he wants. And he's already a doctor. Or he will be, when he passes what he calls his "boards" this spring. Dad was so impressed about that. He heard the text come in while he was helping me import contacts to my new phone. "Dr. Jake." That was all he said, then passed the phone to me. "I'm pleased you gave him your new number, sweetheart."

"Well, he asked for it... in case I have an urgent problem with my stitches," I said.

"Sure, sure." he grinned. "Now that's the kind of man you should be seeing. Someone who runs right for the goal posts. Not someone who fumbles the ball trying to get your attention." I looked down at my phone and Jake's dinner invitation, unsure of what to reply to Dad. We were finally on speaking terms again; I didn't want to lose all the progress we'd made. Still, a big part of me wanted to defend Sam. Dad doesn't know Sam like I know him. He doesn't have a clue about the kind of man he is.

Buggernuts. I can't do this right now. I should definitely have a frank discussion about how my love life is mine and mine alone with my father, but at the moment, I'm about to get stitches again. Before I can ask if it will hurt and how long it will take, Jake has opened the door and is peering out into the hallway. It looks as though he's going to grab the first doe-eyed student who's wandering by. I feel my heart racing and try to remember to breathe.

"Okay, I'm needed elsewhere, catch you later," I hear him call from the hallway. Five minutes pass. I kick my feet back and forth against the examination table. My stitches burn, I have to pee, and my hands are sweaty. More tissue paper ripping. Bloody hell that's an awful sound! Grates on my nerves which are already broken. I could really use a cup of tea right about now.

I'm still fiddling with my side braid, staring at a poster about heart attacks that quite honestly horrifies more than it educates, when Sam steps into the room.

140

# 23 FAULT LINES

## LAUREN

"Oh, it's you."

"Oh, hey," I manage. I let go of my long side braid and sit on my hands.

Sam closes the door. "Jake told me there was a possible duct injury to look at in room four sixty-seven, but I didn't know..." He lets his voice trail off. He looks so serious.

"Duct injury?" I interrupt. "He said it was just going to be re-stitched."

"Yes, but he asked me to call in our ophthalmologist and double-check something else for him too. It's why I called Saif this morning, to bring you in. It's okay, Lauren. The eye surgeon will get you better, I promise."

"You... you suggested Saif drive me in?"

"I thought your eye needed urgent care, that's all. I didn't think it should wait." He doesn't make eye contact. Instead he turns, takes a rolling tray from the corner and wheels it over.

Sam was hurt and angry when he left my place last night, but he still took care of me.

"This will sting just a little." Sam leans in and gently wipes my left eye. Surprisingly, I don't even flinch.

"Sam..." I exhale. I'm not sure where to begin, but we are alone. It's now or never. "I didn't mean to hurt you."

He takes a step back, then reaches down for an instrument, not meeting my gaze. "No problem. We had a couple dates. It's not like we were exclusive or anything." He leans in again and starts to pull out a stitch on the side of my nose. "I'm sure Dr. Jake will show you a good time—he has much deeper pockets. Although, no glowing balls."

The second he says it I can tell he semi-regrets it. I start chuckling.

"I liked your glowing balls lots." I have to say it. He bites his lower lip but miraculously doesn't laugh.

"Sam, it isn't like that. I didn't break up with you so I could see Jake!" He needs to know this.

"I know that, okay?" He puts the black stitches he's just pulled out on the tray, puts down the instrument he was using and pulls off his gloves, tossing them in the garbage bin. "But the Laurens have been trouble from the start. How could you think I was the one trying to profit from what happened? How? I tried to protect you." He's staring at me intently, and I can't take it. Those soulful hazel eyes are brimming with tears.

I stare down at my lap. "I don't know. I was wrong, okay?" I swallow hard. "I was wrong, but it doesn't change us. We're just too complicated."

He starts to open the door. I didn't realize we had so little time.

"Fine, but if you didn't want complicated you probably shouldn't have come to Canada. It snows for seven months, and despite the rumors, no one ever has sex in a canoe. Too tippy." He opens the door farther now and peers out just like Jake did earlier, checking his phone for messages at the same time.

I want to laugh, cry, jump off this ridiculous tissue paper exam table and run to kiss him. From the first moment I met him, it's been the same. He triggers every powerful emotion in me except anger. What am I supposed to do?

My decision is made for me the second Sam returns with another doctor. I feel remorse and then confusion as I hear them speaking.

"It's probably blocked or starting to be blocked. He spoke with you on the day of the surgery though right, so it's probably nothing," Sam says to the white-haired man in a scrub cap. The older doctor is red-faced and sweating furiously, appearing to have just come from surgery.

"No." The doctor is checking his tablet, comparing it against Sam's tablet. "Haven't consulted on this one yet. Only Dr. Marshal's initials here. Just looking at her though, I'd say you're right on the money."

I can't decipher Sam's expression, but I know it's not good. He turns to me and attempts a sideways smile. He looks like that wide-eyed, awkward emoji. Great. Now I know something isn't right.

"Lauren, this is the specialist, Dr. Tremblay. He's going to check to see if your duct is blocked. It can happen when we have surgeries like yours, where the corner of the eye is so close to the stitches on the nose. He'll take this case over from Dr. Marshal, and since he's an eye specialist you should probably see him from now on." He looks distressed. "It's better for everyone..." Before I can even say goodbye, he gives Dr. Tremblay a nod and leaves the room.

I look up at Dr. Tremblay, who is still sweating buckets and let him inspect and then freeze my eye with what he explains is a local anesthetic.

How does Sam always say so much with so few words? Not only is he making sure I'm getting healed, but he's making sure that the chief resident who's dating me doesn't get his hand slapped for doing so. Possibly, he's making sure Jake doesn't get his hand slapped for messing up my stitches when he first inserted them, too. I'm not sure about this, and Sam and I aren't dating anymore, so I can't ask. Still, with all of the *tsk tsk tsking* that Dr. Tremblay is doing right now as he stitches me up again, I think Sam may have just saved my eye as well as his teacher's career.

Dr. Tremblay stops *tsk tsking* and stands back to admire his work. I'm relieved that I hardly felt a thing during his stitching, just slight pressure on the skin and my own emotional torment.

"Well, my dear, we caught it in time." He peers at me above the glasses sliding down the bridge of his nose. "That's quite the promising surgeon you've had working on you."

"Sam? Oh, really?" I'm not sure what else to say.

143

"Yes, I was told at our last board meeting that he's getting his name on a research paper alongside Dr. Marshal. About a rare case of hiccups, actually. Odd but intriguing findings. And it's a first for a non-resident here. This young man's a friend of yours?"

"He is. Er, that is, I'd certainly like him to be." I fumble my response, cough to cover up my awkwardness and am relieved when he stops staring at me, adjusts his glasses and looks back down at his tablet.

Right. I was dating some kind of Canadian superhero, but I've gone and tossed him in the trash can.

There are not enough samosas in the world for this problem, but samosas and wine are where I shall start, the minute I get back to my room.

# 24. THE COLD NEVER BOTHERED ME ANYWAY

**November**

**SAM**

The early morning light cascading through my basement bedroom window warms my face even as the snowflakes fall fast and furious outside, but the rays aren't strong enough for me to see the small sutures I'm sewing into this prosthetic foot. I need to get this perfect so I can ace my surgical exam in two days.

*Buen Dios.* I have spent more time with this plastic foot than I have with any woman. I need to get a life! Even my walk at dawn was cut short because of the snow flurries. I tried to get as far as the park but had to turn back after just five minutes because the wind was blustery.

As I turn on and adjust one of the class surgical headlights, which I was allowed to sign out for twenty-four hours, I wonder if Jake ever went to these kinds of extremes when he was still clerking. Did he work as hard as I've worked? I have to stop my suturing for a second and take deep breaths to calm my anger and disgust. He misses important medical clues all of the time, yet he's going to officially become a doctor this spring. How is this even possible?

I want to report all of the mistakes I've caught, but he's my Chief Resident. I'm supposed to just shut up and do what he says. Everyone in class has stories from years past. The smart kids were the ones who just did as expected. Anyone who tried to think outside the box or point the finger at a superior never graduated.

I want to do the right thing, but I can't disappoint my parents like that, not after all the pain they've endured these last few years. I need to become a doctor, for me first, but also for them. I can only pray that Jake doesn't harm anyone. He should have consulted with an ophthalmologist from the very start. He could have seriously harmed Lauren's eyesight.

Oh, Lauren. What is going on with her? I know the attack must have affected her in ways I can never understand, but I never thought she'd fall for someone like Jake. It's funny; she says it's complicated for us to be together, but she's *making* it complicated. We're so easy together. It isn't work at all. I know she felt that too.

I wipe a bead of sweat off my forehead, adjust my headlamp and continue my interlocking suture across the foot. How am I going to stop wanting her? I'll focus on how much I dislike her. She's opinionated, she cheats at golf games, and she's a little flaky.

But no, that's not really the case. She's simply unsure of what to do. She's been hurt by her parents, her past relationship, and the slime who attacked her. Jake's arrogant, persistent, and used to getting his way. How can I be angry at Lauren for him convincing her that he's what she wants? I can't.

I have to find a way to stop wanting her every damn second of the day. It's been weeks since I saw her last. I have to learn to let her go.

My computer has fallen asleep, and I'd love to do the same. I tap the keyboard to wake it. It's noon already? Between reading my textbook and practicing the suturing, I've been at this for almost four hours.

There's a light tap on my bedroom door. Finally, my parents are learning to knock. They still ask me about my love life all the time, but baby steps. One thing at a time.

I pull off my headlamp and place it on my desk, but don't bother to move my newspapers or the prosthetic foot I'm stitching. Ma has seen it before and is getting used to it. Barely. Dad recently called my bedroom "the cheap horror film in our basement," but he's also adjusting. I swivel my chair around as Ma walks in.

"I made you a sandwich." Ma holds a plate in one hand, tousling my messy locks with the other. "You need to take a break, son." She's made me a sandwich from fresh bread packed with ham, pickles, sweet onions, cumin and melted Swiss cheese. I take the plate, lower my nose for a whiff, and give her a gentle smile. I can't let her know how much this meal makes me think of Lauren. The cumin and sweet onion aroma makes me think of Lauren holding Ma's soup and my wildflowers on her lap during our relaxing truck drive away from campus. It also makes me want to forget about work so I can hang in the kitchen with my parents all afternoon.

"Thanks, but I'm supposed to be at the hospital in an hour." I glance back at the time.

"*Dios.*" She rolls her eyes. "Take a minute to eat first." She sits on the edge of my bed and folds her arms across her chest. "I never see you anymore."

I lean back in the chair and comply. Like I've said before, she usually wins every argument. "I just don't want to miss my lesson with Dr. Pandya. He's the vascular trauma surgeon I like. They usually only let fourth-years scrub-in, but he said I could, to observe his surgery to redirect blood vessels in a patient with poor circulation due to diabetes. I'm so excited to watch and learn."

"One can redirect blood vessels?" Ma shakes her head and exhales. "Yet nothing could save our Sierra." Her eyes lose their vibrant glow.

I take her hand. "Nothing, no. I miss her too, Ma. Every day."

"You spend a lot of time with this... Pandya? He is Muslim doctor, correct?" She looks down at her floor length skirt. She knows I hate it when she tries to do this. She must know I won't let her win this time.

"He is, Ma. He's also wonderfully kind and talented. He took Lauren in when she needed a new place to stay."

147

"Oh goodness, your poor Lauren, she shouldn't be living with those people!"

I stand up and hand her back the bowl. I know I should go wash it up, but she's just lost my respect for today.

"We've been over this, Ma. I don't know what else to say to you about this. It's not like "those people" all share the same traits and ethics. Do all Cubans smoke cigars?"

"Your father doesn't, but..."

"See? You can't lump them into some stereotypical category. I can't believe you still do, when I've become good friends with someone who practices that religion. So what? He didn't kill Sierra, Mother, that isn't on him. That's on the man who decided to drive his van into people that day. His actions that day are his fault alone." I start for the door.

I can hear her beginning to cry behind me, and I don't know what to do. If I put my arms around her, am I allowing her this prejudice? I can't condone it, not even in my mother. I've heard the expression "Each one, teach one," but it's a painful task when the one you're attempting to teach is also your loving parent with whom you empathize.

As the tears start to drip off my mother's chin and she starts making sobbing sounds, I turn from the door, walk back over and wrap my arms around her frail, shaking body. She takes her arms, wraps them around my shoulders and pulls me in closer.

"You're a good man," I hear her whisper between sniffles.

Age is no excuse for closing your mind, but I have faith that my mother's heart is not completely closed. She isn't arguing with me today. Today, she's beginning to let herself feel again.

It takes fifteen minutes to walk to work, but it clears my mind and lifts my spirits. The sky's a celestial blue and the flurries have stopped. It isn't nearly as cold as it was at sunrise. As I get closer to the hospital, I have to zip up the top of my leather jacket, wrap my beige wool scarf around my face and look down at my feet. The wind coming off Lake Ontario is strong.

Once I'm through the parking lot, the wind is blocked by the hospital, and I can look up again. Only, I wish I hadn't looked up.

Jake and Lauren are standing face to face a few meters away from the main entrance. There's a light dusting of snow on the pavement, but Jake is wearing only running shoes, scrubs and a red wool hat. I guess he's on his break and wants to impress Lauren with his bravery by not wearing a jacket when it's fourteen degrees outside. I call that stupidity, but hey, I'm just a dumb med student who co-wrote Jake's research paper.

I exhale to calm the fury I feel inside and watch my breath swirl up into the sky like smoke circles. Now they're laughing together, heads back, hot breath mingling in the cold winter air.

Jake slowly takes off his hat and puts it on Lauren, who's in a red wool jacket but was missing the matching hat. He leans down and kisses her, and I have to look away. Desire and regret and jealousy mingle in my gut, rising to my chest cavity until my heart physically aches. I pull my black hat over my ears and walk past them, head down, before they can notice me.

This is the first snow. Lauren's first snowfall here. He's stolen that from us.

## 25. STAYING IN BED IS THERAPY

### December 11

*Dear Diary,*

*Bloody fracking hell, I need to get a life!*

*It's Friday night, but here I am all alone, sitting cross-legged on my bed in my favorite plaid pajamas, shoving samosas into my face. I'm sure I look like a little chipmunk gathering nuts for winter, but who cares, no one's watching. I just finished studying for two hours for my last exam on Monday, and I have Nietzsche's Daybreak: Thoughts on the Prejudices of Morality, open at page 107 under this diary.*

*I hate to confess this, but since Sam's not here, I can admit to myself how he's right about something. I've grown to love Nietzsche's thoughts. I love how he hated the pretentiousness and closed-minded morality of his time. He fought against the stereotypes and superstitions that prevailed. I can actually relate to a lot of what he said. I'm even considering rereading it, so I know it well enough for April exams.*

*Studying philosophy on a Friday night? Have I gone looney-tunes? Aren't exchange students supposed to come to a new place and meet new people? Aren't we supposed to "party hardy?" I am the most pathetic excuse for a 21-year-old exchange student in the world. All I'm missing is a wicker knitting basket and a cat.*

*The thing is, I'm feeling cozy and at home, and after the attack, I know that's important. My therapist says I need to find ways to feel at home even when I'm not home. She said I have to focus on what makes me feel positive and safe, and then, in time, I won't feel fearful whenever someone's knocking at the door. I love my room, my apple-spice candle, my bed, my sofa under the skylight. On a clear night, I can see the Big Dipper from there. I love not having to open the door for Brittany or wait for her and Lauren J. to use my own mirror. I adore staying home and reading books.*

*I don't enjoy having to dress up for fancy dinner dates with Jake all the time. I hate having to make sure I'm using the right spoon and fork and laughing at the correct spot in his long stories. He is so pretentious.*

I feel my throat grow tight as I write that, so I quickly close my diary and glance at my phone. 10:35 pm. I've completely missed dinner with Jake. When I texted him that I wasn't feeling well, he replied ten minutes later with a poop emoji. A poop emoji? Seriously? I thought he was more mature than that.

I can't take talking to myself any longer. I hope Lexy's awake. It's probably a bad time to Facetime her, but I've already dialed. The call only rings a few times before she answers.

"It's bloody 4 a.m.! This had better be important." She's lying on her bed, wearing a blue sleep mask with FIVE MORE MINUTES sprawled across it atop her forehead. She pulls it back further, so it's resting on top of her blonde hair and glares up at me.

"I was supposed to be on a dinner date with Jake, but I canceled last-minute."

"Wren! I know you're messed up, and you've been through a lot lately, but that was just mean." She frowns at me.

"I just couldn't face him this time. He's almost too perfect. It's hard to be with someone who talks about himself that much. Sam was such a good listener."

"Sam." She pulls off her sleep mask entirely, sits up in bed, and sighs. "For someone you dumped several weeks ago, you're talking about him an awful lot."

"I think about him a lot. But... Dad thinks I should be seeing Jake."

"Tell me this, would you miss him if you stopped dating him?"

"No. Turns out he's a control freak." I exhale loudly, surprised at how quickly I answer this. "But my father..."

"Are you bloody dating Jake or is your father dating him? Because I think your father's hot for him."

"That's not true." I shove half a samosa into my mouth.

"You did the same thing with me, you know. Subconsciously or not, you chose me because of him. As my coach, he was so impressed with my pitching arm in baseball. He practically wanted to be my BFF until he learned I wanted a *yoohoo* where my crotch protection went."

I laugh out loud and small bits of potato goes flying across the room. "Lex. It wasn't quite like that!"

"Was so." She furrows her eyebrows. "I should know. My privates."

She makes me grin big, but I want to address something I haven't been able to before. "I wish I'd known you were going through all of that confusion... so young..." I look at her, studying her face for emotion. She wears no more scars. I'm so relieved we've managed to heal from this.

"We went through it together, and you helped, sweetie. You just didn't really know you were helping. We were so innocent. It was always a friendship more than anything else."

"I know that. And I miss my friend! Can you just forget about your hormone therapy, and exams, and come visit? I'm so lost!" I chuckle at how pathetic I sound as I say it aloud.

"I know, I know—soon. I'd be there tomorrow if you had to testify."

"I'm off the hook, sounds like. Other women came forward. Hank's been in touch with the police. My attacker was a new reporter with *The Edwin Cove Globe*—he even emailed me to get a scoop when my story went viral. He was diagnosed with Sociopathic personality disorder in his teens but kept it on the down-low."

"My God, how did he slip under the radar? Can't they put him away for good yet?" Lexy raises her voice in exasperation. Her eyes are wider than I've ever seen them.

"He had a show-cause hearing, was denied bail and put in secure custody at the hospital to undergo psychiatric evaluation. Hank says they're moving him to Brockville prison before his trial next month. He'll likely be locked up fifty years, if not for life." I wring my hands together and finally remember to exhale. I hate thinking about him and his dark, angry eyes.

"You can breathe easy, sweetie. You've made a difference." Lexy's moved her tablet to her desk and is sitting looking down at me. The soft lighting makes her face look angelic, which I find rather amusing.

"I guess. Something good's come out of it. Almost got blinded but..."

"Your eye looks good."

"Yeah, thanks to Saif and Sam, who insisted I get it looked at."

"There's that name again." She chuckles. "Sam's a diamond in the rough, I tell you. Take a closer look."

"Yeah... if he'll have me back..." I pout.

"Give it time, you never know. So, you're alone there for Christmas? That's gonna suck."

"No, not completely. I think Hank's bringing his family."

"That's great. I wish I could afford a flight out." She starts biting her pinky nail.

"Me too, but I get it," I say, trying to smile at her. I miss hanging out.

"Okay, surprise!" Obviously trying to lighten the mood, she claps her hands together. "I'm sending you something."

"What? Snail mail?"

"Yup. It's supposed to arrive tomorrow. Don't kill me. I just think you could use this. I arranged it all with Saif. It's all good." She winks but it looks like she has dust in her eye. She's a terrible winker, especially when half asleep.

"How the heck does Saif know all my friends?"

"It's a known fact, Indians are the world's best networkers." She chuckles, adding, "I asked Hank for his number, silly!"

"I love you, you noodle. You didn't have to buy me anything."

"Love you more. Now can you bugger off so I can get some sleep?"

## 26. THE ELEMENT OF SURPRISE

### LAUREN

There's a knock on my door, and for the first time in months I jump up out of bed to answer it without a moment's hesitation. The second I do so, I realize what day it is and regret paying any attention to the outside world.

"Argh! It's bloody Saturday morning! Go away! I was supposed to be sleeping in!" I stumble for the door grumbling out loud, momentarily forgetting that Farida or Saif could be on the other side of that door with kind smiles and piping hot samosas. No, I keep forgetting how this room is set up. They'd knock on my inside door, the one that leads to the rest of the house, with those.

I decide to lower my voice a little but can't help mumbling to myself. "I live alone. There's no Brittany to contend with anymore. Yet I'm walking in bare feet to answer the door on a Saturday morning. Some things never change."

"Who's there?" I ask when I reach the door.

When no one answers, I start to feel a little nervous, so I look through the tiny peephole. No one is there. Must be a delivery without a required signature. When I open the door, I look around the corner, down the oak stairs, then behind the door just in case. There's a lone pigeon cooing at me on the bottom step. A mighty gust of wind blows snow on the path in front of him, and he flies away, spooked.

Looking down at the makeshift mailbox I made out of a small wicker basket, I'm expecting to see a letter or small package from Lexy inside. Instead, a medium-sized red cardboard box addressed to me has been placed on the top step. If an Amazon drone left this on a Saturday morning, I need to know how it flew up the stairs, and if Amazon delivers hot breakfasts. I could go for that.

As I pick the box up, step inside and shut the door, the box begins to make noises.

"Mew. Mew."

"Oh no she didn't!" I practically skip to the sofa and sit down with the box on my lap, my heart racing fast. When I do sit, something inside the box moves, and a tiny white paw pokes out of one of the large air holes.

I can't open the box fast enough. Of course, it's taped up like a Mummy, so I have to grab the scissors on the counter across the room and run back to the mewing box to cut the tape.

When all is cut, the kitten practically jumps from the box into my arms. My eyes fill with tears as I lift the fluffy white ball of fur with the hot pink collar to my eye level so that we're staring at one other. Her eyes are Mediterranean Sea blue, and her long white hair looks silky soft. She's stunning, and she smells like freshly folded linen.

"Oh, my goodness, we are going to be forever friends," I squeal as I hold her close to my chest. She's squirming around lots, but I can hear her purring. I pull her back in front of my face again to get another look at her. The small white note card attached to her hot pink diamond studded collar reads:

HALLO! I'M YOUR NEW FLAT MATE!

P.S. SORRY, I KNOW YOU LOVE YOUR SATURDAY SLEEP-IN BUT SAIF COULD ONLY GET TO THE SHELTER AND DELIVER YOU THIS MORNING BEFORE HIS SHIFT.

I chuckle and put the note on the coffee table. Lexy is the master of surprises like this. She knows how sad I was when my parents wouldn't let me get another cat after Princess Leia died. She's a lot like an older sister these days. She gives me tough love all the time, but she obviously worries about my well-being. I'd tell her I'm doing fine, and I don't need a bloody kitten as part of my therapy, in fact, I think I'm finally feeling more like myself these days, but damnit, I want the kitten!

"Are you hungry? I'm sure you were fed at the shelter earlier?" I ask her as if she's going to answer me and check my phone on the coffee table for the time. "Nine a.m. We'll go downstairs and see Farida soon. I'm sure she has bags of food and litter. My three friends have been busy plotting your arrival without my knowledge." I chuckle.

I give her another tight squeeze. "You're going to force me to skip classes just so I can stay home and play with you. You're that adorable!"

"Mew." She licks my chin and it tickles, making me giggle. "I'm glad this term has nearly ended, so we have until mid-January to get used to each other." I hear myself talking out loud to her like she's a person, and I shake my head. I'm an old cat lady, and I'm only twenty-one.

There's a tap on the inside door to my room, and I jump up to answer it. The kitten gets spooked, climbs up my body like it's a tree, and somehow manages to attach herself to my hair.

"Farida!" I say gleefully as I open the door, still trying to pry the kitten off my head. "How did you manage to keep quiet about this…"

It's not Farida.

Sam is standing at the door with a red toolbox in one hand, an empty litter box under his arm, and a tray of coffee cups with the Starry Night Café logo on them.

"Oh, it's you! And I'm in my pajamas. With a cat on my head." I'm not even sure if I say this out loud or not, it's too bloody early in the morning for me to think clearly, but it's Sam, and he gets me. It's fine.

"I'm so sorry, is this an intrusion? Farida told me you were expecting me." He reaches out his arms and offers me the tray of cups. "Earl Grey for you, double mocha for me. I needed a jolt of energy," he says. I put the kitten on the floor behind me, take the litter box and the tray and usher Sam inside.

"Expecting you? I didn't have a bloody clue you were coming. I think Farida is possibly playing matchmaker, just a little." I smirk at him. Those two are something else. They feed me delicious meals, help my friend send me a kitten, and now they're bringing Sam back to me.

"I... I don't know... matchmaker? I'm just here because I owe Saif a favor." He lifts the tool kit with a perplexed look on his face. "I figured enough time has passed that not one reporter would care if I was dropping by your house."

"Oh yes, we are definitely #oldnews. No one's bothered me about the Lauren from Last Night thing in a month. It's such a relief." The second I say it, I feel badly. Not being able to spend time with him hasn't been a relief. It's been more like a necessary evil.

He sighs and closes his eyes for a second, gathering his thoughts. "Um... I don't even think saying "hashtag something" is trendy anymore."

The amused sparkle in his eyes tells me that he didn't take the relief comment the wrong way, and somehow, just by being myself, I've erased the awkwardness of this reunion.

"Just thought you should know, since you're not on social media at all." He winks. "Not that I'm much of an expert myself."

"See? We're in the clear, then," I say, putting the tray of cups on the coffee table and the litterbox in the corner. I take the cup with the little tea label hanging from it and sit beside him on the grey sofa under my skylight. "Thanks for the tea. So, Farida and Saif asked you to come by?"

"Well, Saif did, at the hospital." He puts down his toolkit and leans back into a white cushion on the sofa. "Farida was downstairs cooking, and she just let me in and said you were waiting for me upstairs."

"She did, did she?" I smile and take a sip of the tea. It's made with just the right amount of milk and sugar. I don't remember telling him how I liked it.

"Yeah." When he smiles back at me, it feels like coming home. "I was in surgery with Saif the other day, and..."

"Wait, back up!" I sit cross-legged and pivot my body his way. "That's amazing! You got to do a surgery?"

"Not do it, but I got to observe and hand him tools. It was amazing. I'm learning so much. We were talking after, when we were cleaning up, and I asked how your eye was, how you were..."

"You did?" When I look into his soulful eyes, I don't want to look away.

"Of course, I did. Lauren, I've missed you every day."

"Me too," I say, feeling my throat tighten with emotion.

"You have? But Jake. I've seen you two together..." His voice trails off, and he looks down at his lap.

"We had two dates, that's all. He's not the guy for me, Sam. I've known that for a while." I don't want to hesitate anymore. I don't want to be afraid to love someone anymore. I put my tea down and take his hand in mine. He slowly reaches up and cups my chin, then traces my lower lip with his finger. The feel of his hand on my skin again sends electricity up my spine, across my chest. I lean in and close my eyes, his breath warm on my neck as we let our lips come together. Gripping his shirt, I pull him closer. He tastes like chocolate truffles and feels like Sunday morning, staying warm under the covers.

My new kitten mews and jumps between us.

"Ouch!" Sam mutters. She's landed on his lap. Her nails must be sharp, because Sam bolts up and off the sofa. He starts to chuckle when he realizes it was only a tiny ball of fur that stabbed his thigh, and he picks her up.

"She's certainly full of energy!" He lifts her high above his head. "We'll have to cut your nails, won't we? Won't we?" He's practically purring himself. So, he's a cat person. This is good, but does he have to be a cat person *right now?* I sigh, less about the kitten, more about the lost moment.

"She's cute, but I can tell she's going to be a handful," I say.

"So, this little furball is Lexy's surprise for you." He has her at eye-level and seems as enchanted as I am. "Saif told me all about the plan. I thought it sounded slightly crazy, but then, I haven't met Lexy yet. What's her name?"

"I hadn't decided yet. Want to decide with me?"

"I'd love that." He sighs and pats the kitten. "Maybe a little later, over supper? My work is cut out for me today. I promised to help Saif by putting in a surveillance system. He's in surgery all day, so I've got this."

"A what?" I study his muscular torso, thinking he belongs on a Hot 'n Handy Doctors calendar as he cradles the kitten with one arm and opens the toolbox with his free hand. Inside is a black camera like the kind I've seen in stores, only it's much smaller.

"Saif and I got talking, and with the outside entrance to this room leading right to the street, we thought that installing cameras at the top and bottom of the stairs would be wise. You'll be able to see who's at the door using your tablet. Saif was complaining how he's not much of a handyman, so I offered to help install everything. It's fun and easy for me, and free for him, and besides, I'm all done first term."

I blink and exhale deeply, like one does during a lovely massage. Standing here, just being here with him, I finally feel normal again. Is he for real? "That's really sweet, Sam. I've been doing okay physically, but the door to the outside was frightening me a little. This will really calm my fears." I look at him, tears brimming in my eyes. "Thank you so much for doing this for me."

"Don't thank me yet, I have to take over your stairwell for the morning, and it might be noisy." He bends down and starts rummaging in his toolbox. "Then I'm installing a deadlock bolt on your door to replace that flimsy chain. My father is a little OCD about home security, so he helped me pick one out."

"That's fabulous. I'll brew a pot of coffee. Warm up some samosas. Change out of my PJs while you're in the stairwell." I touch my bottom lip, wondering how to turn back time. I've come alive with the electricity of his kiss, that one finger tracing my lips. I hope he stays all day and night and there are no more interruptions.

"Don't change on account of me." He looks up at me. "I like you exactly how you are."

# 27. WORTH WAITING FOR

## SAM

"You know, I probably could have just done this myself."

Lauren gives me a bright, confident smile and hands me the Phillips screwdriver. I'm on the top rung of a stepladder, desperately trying to get the camera to stay in the right corner of the alcove as I'd imagined it would. This task has proven harder than cross-stitching any prosthetic foot. For the last hour, I've wanted to scream and throw the camera down, but this was supposed to be an exercise in showing Lauren I'm the patient, mature man she wants to be with, not the childish perfectionist I know I can be at times.

"You absolutely could have, and possibly far better than me, but then you wouldn't have learned the finest Spanish swear words in the world." I wink at her over my shoulder, then turn back to the wiring job. I'm trying not to picture her in my mind so I can concentrate on the work, but that lilac fitted top under her distressed denim overalls and the way her eyes light up when she looks at me—not so easy to forget.

"'*Hostia!*' was an interesting choice, and I like how you contorted your face and neck like an old tortoise when you said it," Lauren says.

"My neck looked like a tortoise's? When does one ever see what that looks like, if tortoises are always inside their shells?" I'm laughing with her and a little concerned I'm going to topple off the ladder if I'm not careful.

"I've gotten a good look. I bloody like spending time at the zoo, okay?" She leans forward and grins up at me. "Lately, I've realized I prefer animals to most people. They don't have opinions on everything. They don't talk back."

"I know what you mean," I concur. "We'll have to go sometime, then. There's one in Toronto." I surprise myself as I say it. I haven't been outside Edwin Cove for years because the thought of going back to the city where Sierra was murdered has terrified me and my parents. But now, I have someone to take back there. Lauren and I can make happier memories there.

"Bangin' idea. I love it," she says, steadying my ladder with both hands. "Let's go as soon as exams are over in April."

One more twist of the Phillips... there. I lift my hands off the installed camera and take a look. I may have figured this out.

"I think it's finally going to work. Let's go take a look." I jump off the last rung of the stepladder, and I motion to Lauren to walk ahead of me.

"Let's hope, it's almost six, and I can smell Farida's cooking. That strong cumin aroma always travels far," Lauren says as she moves inside and walks over to her sofa.

As I close the door, it hits me that I didn't feel nervous being out there at dusk as I usually do. They say time heals all wounds, but I don't quite believe that. I think it takes special people to come into your life to guide you through the healing. As they reveal their love for you, your scars become smoother, less rough at the edges. Old scars never disappear but fade with the shift of time and the sway of love. I bow my head as I sit beside Lauren on the sofa, silently thanking her and my friend Saif for giving me this new strength, this new confidence. Sierra probably had a whole lot to do with this, too. I thank her in my prayers every night.

"You alright?" Lauren asks softly.

"I'm more than alright." I lift my head, then turn Lauren's tablet on the coffee table so she can see the screen. "It's been a great day."

"It really has. I didn't know just completing a chore like that could be so much fun," she says. "And we even named the little sweetheart, didn't we, Snowflake?" She gives the purring white kitten at her feet a pat.

"Well, I thought my suggestion of Nietzsche was brilliant," I say. "Bit of a mouthful, though. Snowflake is much cuter."

She nods, then leans in closer to me and studies the tablet. "Look at that! That's the stairwell leading to my door. I can even see down the sidewalk, around the corner!" She grabs my hand and gives it a squeeze, beaming. "It's just what I needed."

"You can thank Saif for the idea; I just installed it," I say. "You have yourself some wonderful landlords."

"I know, what a switch from residence. I'm so spoiled." Just as she says it, there's a tap on her door. I hear Farida's gleeful voice. "Hello? I made samosa tacos and chutneys."

"Come in, come in!" Lauren says, jumping to her feet to open the door to the house. "See what I mean?" She laughs as Farida strolls inside, holding a pink glass plate covered in a beautiful array of what looks like homemade potato and cilantro tacos.

As Lauren sits back down beside me, Farida places the plate before us, then stands back and claps her hands together. "My handy workers. Eat. Eat! Saif will be working late, and I had some already." She looks over at me and gives me a wink. I can't believe she just did that in front of Lauren. I bite my lower lip and try not to chuckle.

"Farida, you should sit and join us. All of this work!" I motion for her to sit beside us.

"No, no, I made them weeks ago, I just reheat the tacos and filling. Not a problem. You kids eat, have a nice date!" She winks again, this time at Lauren, then walks briskly to the door, her gold bangles jingling a melodic tune as she leaves.

"Did we seriously just eat all of that?" I lean back into the comfy white pillow, Lauren's head resting on my chest as we stare at the empty pink plate and the small, nearly empty bowls of cilantro chutney and tamarind chutney. Lauren lit a candle when it got dark out—I think it was called What a Pear—and now the flickering flame and melding of Indian spices with the light scent of pears is almost as intoxicating as this small glass of California shiraz.

"We did. We should probably go to the gym over the holidays." Lauren chuckles and snuggles in closer. Of all the scents in this room, her vanilla-mandarin fragrance is the one that's really doing me in. I lean forward, put down my red wine and turn to face her.

"You just said 'we' again. You've been saying 'we' all day."

"Do you have a problem with that?" she asks gently. "I kind of like the sound of it."

"I love the sound of it." I stroke her cheekbone with my thumb, then cup her face with my hand and pull her lips to mine. She melts into me, running her hands through my hair. She's so close to me I can feel her chest moving against mine as she breathes, her eyelashes fluttering against my eyelids. Our kiss is like being inside a house on fire; it's so intense, I know I need to pull away. As I start to move from her, she places her hands on my chest to stop me, snaps off the denim straps to her overalls and pulls off her top and bra. I inhale, then exhale deeply and just sit here blinking, lost in a stupor, lost in her beauty. She tugs at the elastic in her braid and shakes her hair loose. Seconds later, her dark hair is full, cascading down her candlelit breasts and bare shoulders. She pulls off my t-shirt, leans back against the length of the sofa and pulls me down with her. Her delicate features are glowing in the flickering orange light, her eyes luminous. They hold a lustful look I've never seen before.

"You came back for me," she whispers. "I wish I hadn't been so stupid."

"Shhh. We were both stupid." I kiss her eyelids, the tip of her nose, her neck, then let my lips travel across her collarbone. Running my hands down the length of her body, resting one at the small of her back, she starts to moan ever so quietly. As I caress her lower back and kiss her collarbone, her moaning turns into an adorable kind of purring, which turns me on even more.

"Sam... I want to. I want to so much," she says, sounding breathless. "I've just never..."

"Me neither," I say, not hesitating.

"Wow," she says, not judging, just taking it in. "I thought maybe... 'cause you're older..." she whispers, looking up at me. "How come?"

"I guess..." I close my eyes, trying to contain my emotion. When I open them, she's looking right into me, tears streaming down her cheeks. Wiping her tears away with my finger, I kiss her once more.

"I was just waiting for the right one." I say.

# 28. OVERSTOCK OF JOY

## LAUREN

Early morning rays shine through the skylight above the sofa, gently waking me from a deep sleep. The room's light is white and hopeful like a clear morning in May; the air smells of oranges, cumin, a hint of red wine. I feel a strong, warm arm across my chest and look to find Sam's peaceful face close to mine, reassuring me that this is not a dream. Reaching over to where I left my phone on the coffee table, I tap it to wake it up: 9:45 a.m. I don't bloody believe it. We slept in. I got several beautiful hours of sleep last night! Not only is Sam a wonderful person, but he's going to become a brilliant surgeon, he can fix things, and best of all, he loves sleep as much as I do.

Snowflake mews and leaps up to join us, skirting across Sam's legs and torso as she chases a ray of sunlight on the white throw that covers us. Smiling to myself with what feels like an overstock of joy, I sit up and give her a pat, recalling the details of our beautiful night which elapsed into the small hours of the morning.

We must have fallen asleep here. I remember now. We were holding each other, talking about how we'd never felt more loved in our lives, and then Sam asked me, could we make up for the lost time together? He wondered if I could find work and stay in Edwin Cove this summer, so we can enjoy the lakeside festivities when most of the students have left town and it's a different vibe—plus, much warmer. I love the idea and already know where I can apply for work. Saif and Farida were asking me about my interests over dinner last week, and I told them I wished I'd considered Psychology more seriously back in the UK. My coursework here has convinced me I'm quite interested in the mind and how it works, and since my attack, visits with my therapist, June, have piqued my interest. Saif told me that June often takes on a summer student in her office at the hospital, to answer the phones and do filing so she can take Tuesdays and Fridays off. I've already signed a lease to stay a full year in this apartment, so now I won't have to sublet it this summer. I'm excited to make this happen. My CV is updated and typed up. I did that last Friday night after my chat with Saif; I fully admit that I have a quirk wherein I feel compelled to be a total nerd on Friday nights. I may need to speak with my therapist about this need to achieve. No I'm not kidding—she has me opening up about everything, including my unhealthy obsession with royal weddings—but she's taking time off until the New Year. I'll slip a copy of my CV under her door as soon as I can get to the hospital.

"Good morning, beautiful," Sam whispers, caressing my back in small circles. I pull up the throw, so it covers us completely, lie back down and face him.

"Hi. Fancy meeting you in a place like this." I giggle.

"All we need is a beer shower to make this moment complete," he says.

"No, thank you very much!" I kiss him hard on the lips, and he responds by pulling me closer to his warm chest. This is the best way to wake up. I can't believe I didn't know it could be this good. As the seconds melt into minutes, I'm lost in us, lost in a dreamlike state. Then Snowflake jumps on my back, pulling me away from it.

"Ow!" I sit up quick and put the kitten down on the floor. "I'll have beef with Lexy about this. I know she was trying to give me a companion, but did my companion's nails have to feel like a surgeon's knife?"

"Wren." He rubs my back where the kitten slashed it, and I melt, realizing he's just used the nickname Lexy created for me. Somehow, I love it even more coming from him. "She meant well, first off, and secondly, what do you have against surgeons?"

"Oh, nothing at all, as long as they're good." I laugh and lean in to kiss him.

"I'm getting there. I think under Saif's counsel, I will be, some day." He looks so modest in this moment I wish I could record it: the way his eyes are closed; his pensive brow and strong jawline. He's already saved lives, but he's still trying to better himself.

"Do you want me to put a bandage on that cut?" he asks, sitting up to study it closer.

"No, no, it's nothing, not deep at all." I find my lilac shirt on the floor and pull it back on, then stand. The shirt only just covers the top of my bum, but I feel so comfortable around Sam already, I don't care. I see a sparkle in Sam's eyes as he reads the back of my black panties: GRUMPY BUT GORGEOUS.

"Don't say it. I know it's spot on," I say.

Sam is biting his lower lip, his eyes wide with amusement. "I agree with the last part," he says rather diplomatically.

"I have to feed Snowflake." I pick up the samosa plate and a wine glass off the coffee table. Can I make you a tea? I don't have any mocha coffee, sorry."

He pulls on his t-shirt and tousles his hair. In this moment, he's another stunning calendar page of perfection: toned abs and thighs, draped in a white throw, basking in the sunlight on my sofa.

"I'd love to try Earl Grey," he says. "A first time for everything."

He smiles at me, and I head to my electric kettle on the counter. Once it's on, I turn and lean against the counter edge, taking in the sight of him. Relaxed on the sofa, he's patting Snowflake in his muscular arms, sunlight streaming in from the skylight above. I feel my throat tighten with emotion. I've definitely been given an overstock of joy, but I'm keeping it, and I'm not questioning why it's mine. I deserve it.

I was so wrong about love. After Dad and Mum split up, I started believing that lasting love isn't possible. That it's just a concept we all strive for as we scroll down the flawless, white-toothed couples on social media, but we aren't all given a chance at it.

Now I understand. There's no scarcity of love in the world; only scarcity of resolve to accept that love. That's the kicker. It's frightening to accept something as powerful as unconditional love into your heart, to take it with gratitude and without expectations, to allow it to grow in its own magical, meandering way.

As I shuffle over to my Sam with two steaming mugs of Earl Grey, I realize I'm finally ready to accept love. Bring it on. Bring it all. I'm open to the adventure. But first, tea.

# 29. REVELATIONS

## LAUREN

After we've dressed and lingered over our late breakfast of tea and scones, Sam asks if I've read the handwritten letter he gave me yet. I feel ashamed to have simply tossed it aside on moving day and never opened it after that. I can't even meet his eyes. He walks to the side table where the letter is stacked on top of some textbooks and other mail, picks it up and comes to sit close beside me on the sofa.

"Could I read it to you now?" he asks gently.

"I'd love that. Maybe I just wasn't ready for what that letter had to reveal about me, or about us, not then. But I am now," I say.

He clears his throat, unfolds the letter, and begins to read.

> Lauren,
>
> I learned from my own bumbling mistake that there are at least 245 other women with your name at this university, but I've never met anyone like you. You're fiercely independent, private, even, yet you make friends quickly when you trust someone. Saif tells me that you're already close with Farida and you haven't even moved in yet. You're clever, funny, and brave. I also think you're gorgeous, and your accent enchants me.
>
> Somehow, I managed to get the whole town, and maybe half the world's attention, but all I really want is your attention. I want to get to know you better, in private, without the

online world watching our every move. Would you please give us another chance?

With love and admiration,

Sam

"Oh, Sam," I sigh, leaning in to hold him close. "I wish I'd read this earlier. Yes, yes, let's have a good old-fashioned private love affair." As I say it, Sam's eyes twinkle with delight and mischief.

"How about a private dinner here tonight, but a public walk to the hospital now? I'm almost late for my rotation," he says.

"I'd love that," I say. "I can hand in my CV that way and have a talk with Jake."

"There are things to say to Jake?"

We slip on our boots and coats and leave the apartment, locking the outside door behind us.

"I just think I owe him an apology for canceling our last date," I say, starting down the steps. "And make sure he knows we're a thing."

"Okay, but go easy on him. He's been in a rotten mood the last few days."

"Oh? Do you think it's about me?"

"Not just you. He's being assessed by the Royal College of Medicine, and I don't think it's going well."

"The Royal College?" I've never heard of that.

"They assess his postgraduate training so he can be certified in Vascular surgery. Word around the locker room is he didn't pass the assessment." He doesn't sound at all smug, like some would, like I believe Jake himself would if the situation were reversed. He's simply telling me the facts.

"Did you speak to the College about Jake's lax attitude toward my eye?"

"I didn't, I swear. But yours wasn't his only preventable mistake, and karma has a way of giving people a good swift kick in the ass when they need one." He reaches out for my hand as I make my way down the last step to the sidewalk.

The snow sparkles in the Sunday afternoon light, reflecting hues of sea blue. I kick up the tips of my boots to watch the powdery snow spray in front of us, forging a path through Battlefield Park.

"Hey, careful, you'll get your pants all wet!" Sam's laughing. "You're such a little kid." He squeezes my hand, and I squeeze back, thrilled to finally be walking together in a winter wonderland, just like the song. There are, of course, cars honking, pumping exhaust into the cold air on the road that lines the park, but other than that, it's a near perfect stroll under snow-laden pines and antique streetlamps.

At the front of the hospital, Sam bends to give me a long kiss, then checks his phone. "A gentleman always walks his lady to her destination, but this time..."

"I'm fine," I chuckle. "I know where I'm going. You're late!"

"Yeah, it's a good thing I'm now on Saif's rotation," he says. "He may be slightly more lenient with me being late than Jake was, knowing I'm falling in love with his adorable British tenant."

I feel slightly unbalanced but joyful as I hear him say it out loud. "I'm falling, too, but don't be a slacker on account of me," I reply. "As Farida says, go save lives." I point to the Emergency entrance.

He gives me one more kiss, then turns and runs through the sliding glass doors, calling back over his shoulder. "We were up until two, Wren. I think today is just about getting through this shift. See you tonight!"

# 30. SURPRISE VISIT

## LAUREN

As the glass doors slide closed and Sam disappears from view, the wind picks up, and I need to cover my face with my red wool scarf. Pulling some of the wool down to try to see where I'm walking, a sheet of drifting snow nearly blinds me. I blink away the snowflakes, press the envelope for June against my chest, rush around the corner to the hospital's main entrance revolving door and give it a push. Once inside, I take off my mitts, shove them in my pocket and look around for a place to sit where I can write June's full name on my manila envelope.

The flower arrangements in the lobby don't smell like flowers, they smell like lemons and mouthwash. Or maybe that's the freshly cleaned floors which are still damp, so I have to watch my step. No one else seems to notice the slippery floors. The place is a bustle of activity, with people coming and going through the doors to the reception desk. In a waiting area to the left a woman announces last names and numbers on the loudspeaker. Her voice cracks when she speaks, and by her raspy tone I assume she smokes at least three packs of cigarettes a day. I know she's supposed to sound efficient, but to me, she just comes off as angry, and it makes me chuckle to myself.

What she says: "Thirty-two."

What I hear: "If you don't get your fat ass up here soon, I am going to kill you."

There's a digital sign displaying the called numbers in red above several occupied chairs. Slipping off my coat and leaving it on the one available chair at the far wall, I hear someone call my name and look up, confused.

"Wren!"

I can't believe my eyes. It's Lexy. My dear friend is running to me, sporting newly-dyed, short pink hair, purple lipstick, a black fedora, shiny black leggings under a little grey skirt, and a black shirt with white font that reads:

"YEAH. SO?"

She's finally come to see me! I run to meet her at the center of the lobby, pulling her in for a hug. After our long embrace, she leaves her hands at my elbows and starts jumping up and down and squealing in excitement. She's much taller and more muscular than me, so with the momentum she has going, I can't help but jump along with her. Her appearance is markedly different from last spring, and yet, when I look in her eyes, when I hear her laugh, she's still my good friend Lexy.

"You have boobs!" I can't help but whisper in her ear.

She nods and starts to giggle.

"Bangin' right? Am I hot stuff or what?" she says, stopping dramatically to strike a pose, hand on hip. "Estradiol injections. The first few weeks I was a nauseous wreck, but I'm getting used to them now."

"You must be freezing!" I glance at her legs and skirt, pulling her away from the center of the room, closer to the far wall. "Did you even realize it's December in Canada, Lex?"

"I know, a tad underdressed, but my coat's at your pad. Got an Uber from the airport to your place, and when your friend Farida told me where you were, I came here right away. Couldn't wait." She smiles at me and gives me a squeeze, her arm around my waist.

"I have to drop off this CV and then we can go. Come with?" I ask, already starting for the C wing. She nods and follows.

"You're applying for work here?" she asks as we turn a corner into B wing.

"Summertime. I want to stay here... with Sam." I grin at her and can't contain a giggle.

"You're with Sam now? That was fast! Tell me everything!" she squeals as we pass by several examination rooms.

"I haven't. It just happened. Just last night." I sigh.

"Bloody hell, that's fantastic! We have so much to catch up on," she enthuses, lowering her voice as we arrive at a group of quiet offices in C wing. "I'm here for two weeks, if you'll have me."

I stop walking and turn to her, a little breathless. "It's perfect. You can get to know Sam. Mum and I still aren't talking, and Dad's spending Christmas with Denise and her daughter. You two can be my family." It's a bittersweet thought, and I have to take a deep breath and swallow hard to stop myself from tearing up. Hank said he might be bringing his family for a couple days on Christmas. I hope he can make it because my first Christmas in Canada wouldn't be the same without him.

"I'm so sorry, Wren. Give it time. Maybe your mum needs to find out what she's missing. Although, frankly, I think she's going through a mean bitch phase." She puts her right arm around my shoulder as we saunter further down the hall. My eyes scan the doors for June's name. I'm sure we're quite a sight to those not accustomed to seeing pink-haired transgender women roaming the hospital halls, but I don't bloody care. My friend has come to spend time with me. It's just what I need.

"She's being selfish because she feels it's warranted," I say. "As a woman in medicine, it's taken her far longer to get to where she is in her career compared to Dad. Women need to be ruthless to make something of themselves, today. I just never thought my own mother would do this to me." I exhale as the words spill out of me and realize how talking with Lex is even better than therapy. It feels good to be reminded that no matter how bad life gets, I'll always have a handful of loyal friends I can turn to.

"Here we are, this is what I'm looking for. Dr. June Lowry's office." I give the doorknob a turn. It doesn't open.

"Just as I thought, she's started holidays. I'll just slip this under the door." I do exactly that and turn to leave with Lexy in tow when I remember I wanted to speak with Jake.

"Damn, Lex, I need to see if I can find Jake. Sorry but it's important that I speak with him. He's probably around the ER or in an exam room. I'll text him and see if he replies. Why don't you go back to the lobby and wait for me? I'll show you around town once I'm done."

"I can tag along... unless you don't want me here?" she says as I pull out my phone and start texting Jake.

"No, no." I take her hand and give it a squeeze. "I'm elated that you're here, but I should talk to Jake in private. You can stay in the hall, no probs." As I respond to her, my phone pings. That was quick! Jake's usually too busy to reply.

<102 91> Is all his text says. Sam warned me that Jake was moody lately, but I didn't expect him to be this curt. I guess I have some apologizing to do.

"Weird. Okay, let's try one-oh-two." I glance at the number on the door beside me. It's ninety-eight. "I think he's just around this corner."

The door to room 102 is slightly ajar, and as I come closer, I hear Jake's distinctly deep voice talking to someone in a calming tone. Lexy motions that she'll just wait in the hall. The old wooden door creaks as I push it open and step inside.

Jake is standing in the corner beside an empty examining table. His phone is lying at the center, far from his reach.

"Talking to yourself? Job's finally gotten to you, has it?" I tease, hoping to ease into my heavier announcement that we can't see each other anymore.

"Yeah, long day. Look, you should go." He stares at me, not blinking. This can't be simply anger. He looks terrified. His left fist holds a silver pair of surgical scissors, but he's gripping them more like a weapon than a surgical tool, and beads of sweat are dripping from his brow, trickling down his jawline.

The door slams shut behind me. I briskly turn to see who closed it and find myself staring into the barrel of a pistol.

When I see those dark, menacing eyes, I gasp out loud. The man holding the gun has the face I thought I'd nearly erased from my memory.

"Hello, Lauren. Been looking for you." He sneers at me and pulls back the slide on his gun. "You, little girl, made me lose my job."

Heather Grace Stewart

# 31. KILLER INSTINCTS

## SAM

"Sam! Quick, it's Lauren."

Ronny grabs me by my arm and pulls me down the empty hospital corridor. My classmate, Lucy, is running behind Ronny, in turn attempting to keep him back by pulling the back of his scrub shirt. A tall woman with pink hair and a black fedora is showing Ronny the way, begging for us all to hurry.

"Ronny, stop it! Leave this to security and the police, they've been called. We should run for cover." Lucy's eyes are wide, her voice uneven.

Ronny breaks free of her grasp and we keep on running, leaving her at ER reception.

"Lauren? Police? *Dios.*" I don't need to be pulled now. I'm sprinting down the corridor in the direction Ronny's taking me.

"She's been taken hostage by a psych ward patient. Guard's some ancient guy. We think he nodded off. Came up on the guard from behind, took a scalpel to his neck, stole his gun and some scrubs and escaped down the stairs."

The pink-haired woman cries, and when I look in her eyes, I recognize her from Lauren's photos as Lexy.

"How in hell?" I can't get my questions out. I can't even breathe. How did this happen? A hospital, my hospital, is supposed to be the safest place in town, but a crazy person got a gun, and now and he's got my girlfriend.

"They're in this room, but he's locked it."

"Sam! Wait for the police!" I hear Saif calling to me from down the hall, but instead of his familiar voice holding me back, it jolts me into

185

action. It makes me think of Lauren; how scared she must be right now, and how I have to act fast, faster than I did when Sierra was hit by the van. As fast as I can. Not listening to anyone's words of warning, not thinking, I kick open the door. The second I do I hear a gun go off. He's shot through the roof, narrowly missing me.

"This is perfect. Now I can kill you and your boyfriends." The red-faced man snarls, then spits at me. He's got Lauren in a firm grip with his left arm tight around her waist. She's weeping; her hands trembling.

"Shoot me. Shoot me instead." As I shout at him, Jake sprints out of the room, diverting the attacker's attention. I lunge for his gun, and as we struggle with it close to our bodies, he lets Lauren loose. The gun goes off... once... twice. The sound is alarmingly loud; the strong smell of gunpowder makes me feel ill.

The shooter's down, not moving. *Dios,* did he shoot Lauren? I've lost my breath and have an unstoppable need to close my eyes. *No! Please, no. Let her be safe.*

Feeling intense pressure and a burning sensation in my abdomen, I look down to see bright red blood spurting out from under my scrub shirt. *Hostia.* I cover the bullet wound with both hands, then slide down the wall to a crumpled heap on the floor. All my thoughts fade to nothingness.

"Left quadrant bullet wound, severe bleeding, sepsis from the descending and sigmoid colon. Uncertain if he got the spinal cord. Don't move him until we know."

*Am I dead?* I can't open my eyes or lips to speak, but I hear Jake shouting my status to other doctors and possibly paramedics who've arrived in the room.

"We've pushed hemostatic tissue into the wound," Jake speaks nervously to someone, and I'm filled with gratitude when I hear it's my friend Saif responding.

"Good Jake, you did good. You three, lift him on the board please, he's going into hemorrhagic shock. OR two, stat."

I feel hands under me as my back slides onto a flat board, but I can't see or speak to anyone. I try speaking Saif's name, but it comes out jumbled, if at all.

"Saif... Lauren..." I try once more, and this time he hears me. I feel a hand squeezing mine.

"She's good Sam. Focus on you. Stay awake, stay with us, we all need you to stick around," Saif says in a calm, even tone.

Relief washes over me as I hear Lauren's not injured. I try once more to open my eyes, but they're so heavy, and I'm so very tired. I can't stay awake. I give up. I give in.

*Dios.* Such bright lights shining on my face. I'm in surgery already? I wish Saif would lower the strength of his head light. And all this noise. Suction, more suction, shouting, drilling. This is not helping me sleep.

Who's there?

*Sam, you need to fight. You need to live. Ma and Pa need you. They're finally doing better, the family's healed. And you've found love! You have so many more walks on the edge, my dear brother. Don't give up. Choose the adventure that is life.*

## 32. LA FAMILIA

**LAUREN**

"Sam," I whisper his name as I gently stroke his thick, wavy hair. "Please, please wake up."

Though it's after noon, Sam's hospital room is dark. Mrs. Sanchez drew the long, green shades when Dr. Pandya said it would be better for Sam to rest in a cool, dark environment. I was getting used to the hospital's stale peppermint candy scent, but far stronger aromas overpower that now that Lexy, Mrs. Sanchez, Farida and I have practically set up camp in this room. Earl Grey tea with milk and cookies, samosas, and black bean soup permeate the air, mingling with light perfume from the sweet yellow rose arrangement sent by Sam's classmates.

I've had a lump in my throat for twenty-four hours, but it doesn't feel foreign anymore. It's a part of me. I thought I'd cried all the tears I have left in every pore of my body, but it seems there are still more behind that hard lump.

I turn around to Sam's mother, and she puts her arms around me in a tight embrace. What an awful way to have met his parents. Her lower lip starts to quiver, and I know what's coming.

"My boy!" Her body shakes as she emits small sobs. She looks over my shoulder at his still, sleeping body. "He can't sleep forever. Dr. Pandya said so. He said!" Much shorter than me, she's crying into my chest.

"Saif said the anesthesia was a bit strong for him, and his brain just needs to get back to its normal chemistry," I say softly as we continue hugging. "It's going to be fine," I tell her, not believing my own words.

"Sam would tell you it's going to be fine." There, now I believe what I'm saying.

"Maybe we should go to the cafeteria, get more milk and tea bags?" Lexy suggests. She's been quietly sitting in the corner chair, checking the time on her phone.

I give her a thankful nod. "I think my family should be here in an hour, and maybe then we can all have some supper?"

I don't know how I'm finding this inner strength to sound positive and just go with the flow. Perhaps it's because yesterday Mrs. Sanchez gave me strength when I could no longer stand; now it's my turn to do the same for her. I pat her back, and as we both pull away from our embrace and look at one another, I try my best to give her a reassuring look. I feel thankful that my parents are flying in together to support me, but it's amazing how a near stranger can give you strength in times like these.

Yesterday, Mrs. Sanchez gave everyone who visited Sam some black bean Cuban soup. Despite my deep sadness, watching her serving bowl after bowl of that out of a big plastic container made the corners of my mouth lift just a little. Mr. Sanchez told me all about the different varieties of bulbs he planted last fall in the garden and how Sam needs to wake up to make me bouquets with them this spring. That man exudes good faith. Mrs. Sanchez told me to call her "Ma" as we shared our first bowl of black bean soup. It may be too soon to use that name, but I know that whatever happens, I have another family to turn to.

"Sure, we go, Carlos is there, we'll go see him." Grief consumes her face. She looks like she can barely walk. Seeing this, Lexy stands and we take her by the elbow and start to lead her out of the room.

"So, so hungry. Where's my soup?" The raspy voice behind me has that familiar hint of mischief to it, and it's a voice I've grown to love. I briskly turn to find Sam's eyes open.

"Ma! He's awake! He's awake!" I cry, and she turns to face her son, covering her mouth with her hands.

*"Dios Santo en el cielo!"* When she sees her son's eyes are open, she cries and raises her arms to the heavens.

## 33. ILLUMINATION

**SAM**

"Don't you bloody scare us like that ever again, Sam Sanchez, do you hear me?"

Lauren's wet cheeks and eyelashes brush against mine as she kisses my lips for what feels like the fourteenth time, but I don't mind one bit. This moment feels warm and hopeful, like clouds bursting forth summer rain, ending the dry spell. If my abdomen didn't feel like a semi-truck had driven over and through it, I'd pick Lauren up and twirl her around the hospital room with giddy abandon.

"Well, well, Sam, you decided to rejoin the waking world." Saif's sporting his blue turban, scrubs and a huge grin on his face. He rushes up to my bed behind Ma, who, after planting her twelve dozen kisses on my cheeks and forehead earlier, ran to get Saif and Pa and tell them the good news. As Saif offers me his hand and I take it, I pull him in for a hug, slapping him on the back.

"Lauren just told me how you saved my life," I say, choking back tears. "Thank you, Sir. You're a true *amigo*, and the best surgeon we have."

"You're lucky I did anything for you, after that dumb-ass stunt you pulled!" I've never heard him swear before, and it makes me want to laugh, but I'm not sure I'm allowed to with my bandaged abdomen. If he and Farida ever have children, he'll be the softie. I know this because while he's glaring at me, the sparkle in his eyes holds true affection.

Kicking down that door! Diving for a gun!" He shakes his head as he says this and gets Ma all excited in the process. She's nodding and *tsk tsking* along with him.

"Dr. Pandya." She takes both his hands in hers.

"Call me Saif," he says without hesitation, his brown eyes brimming with tears. "Your son is my colleague and my friend."

"Saif," she smiles through her own tears, "you are my hero. You're a tremendous doctor, a tremendous man. Thank you for saving my boy's life." She pats the top of his hand. "You will be our guest for a meal sometime soon." She says this firmly, not leaving the offer open to negotiation.

Saif is visibly moved; I hear him sigh as he wipes a tear off his cheek. Ma reaches up, pulls his forearms closer to her and gives him a hug. As Pa enters the room, his eyes widen at the sight of Ma and Saif in their embrace.

"Well, there you go. People change. The world can change." My father says this rather emphatically but to no one in particular, then walks to my bed and gives me a firm handshake and a sideways hug.

"My son, don't be a hero like that again. You must take care of those surgeon hands. You'll be needing them in the future. And not just for repairing rubber feet. I hear you're good in emergencies." He pulls out of the hug, his wrinkled eyes crinkling with pride and admiration. I'll never forget this look on his face.

Suddenly, I feel dizzy and slightly nauseous. It's all coming back to me. "I killed someone. He's dead, isn't he?" I look up into Saif's eyes.

"Yes, Sam, but he was a very dangerous man..." he replies.

"You saved my life, Sam." Lauren takes my hand in hers and gives it a squeeze. "He very nearly took mine. The police say that Braden Price was obsessed with me. They dug around, found he'd been following and sharing our story closely through his many Twitter accounts and bots." She shudders. "But he's gone now." As she says it, she exhales and squeezes my hand harder. "Thanks to you."

"If you hadn't shot him, I would have, but I faint at the mere sight of a needle, so I don't think I'd have survived a gunshot!" Lexy has come up beside Lauren and Ma. She lowers her black fedora with one hand and gives me a nod.

"Lexy, it's good to finally meet you," I say. "Sorry for the strange circumstances..."

"Don't worry about it, all the excitement around here makes my life feel rather 'normal!'" She makes the quote unquote gesture with her hands, then chuckles, and it makes me smile.

I don't dare laugh because Saif is already fast at work, checking my vitals with nurse Julie by his side. He's lifting my hospital gown, taking a closer look at the dressing on my wound.

"So, the wound looks good, but you're on IV for possible infection. By some miracle, we avoided sepsis. Your bowel was perforated, and I had to repair it and other vascular tissue. One surgery is likely adequate, but we're keeping an eye on you. One more week in hospital, then if no fever or other complications, we'll send you home.

"By the twenty-fifth?" I feel relief wash over me. I'm determined to get better in time for my first Christmas with Lauren.

"I'll see what we can do. No promises," he says, patting my shoulder. "Now, rest up. You mustn't get an infection."

Visiting hours are nearly over, so with the help of Lauren's clever sidekick, Lexy, giving out strong "we should leave" signals—she offered to buy everyone pie at Starry Night Café—our families have left us alone for the night. Must remember I owe Lexy one, although I get the feeling she isn't the type to keep tabs.

Nurse Julie rushes into the room and pulls out my dinner tray, then places three different Jell-O's on it.

"There. Do me a favor?" she says, her voice a near whisper.

"Anything!" I say, ravenously digging into the cherry Jell-O. I despised the rice and curry chicken I was given for supper and begged Julie to bring me extra desserts.

"Eat them quickly. Destroy all the evidence." She grins and gives me a high-five, then winks at Lauren and bustles out of the room.

"Want some?" Lauren shakes her head, then sits on the top edge of my bed, right beside me, and I wonder if we can find room for her to lie down here with me. Just as I'm leaning back on my pillows about to ask her to cuddle with me, Jake flies into the room, his eyeballs nearly bulging out of his skull.

"Look, I know you got hurt Sam, okay, but I'm pissed you'd break the code." He crosses his arms over his chest and glares at me. He doesn't even acknowledge Lauren is here.

"The code?"

"Yeah, the code. I just got a notice from the Royal College of Medicine who were assessing my postgraduate training so I could be certified in vascular surgery. I didn't pass the assessment. They think I need another year of residency, and that I should just concentrate on general surgery." His left hand is clenched in a fist.

"Oh, that's a shame," I say, only half meaning it.

"Yeah well, interestingly enough, or not, Dr. Pandya—our new Chief of Surgery and a vascular surgeon, may I add—" he furrows his brow and clears his throat, "is on the board at the College. I wonder what a little bird told him."

"Jake. I didn't!" I sit up fast, and the exertion hurts, making me groan out loud. Lauren gently eases me back to a more relaxed position. "I wouldn't!" I continue, trying to control my voice and temper so that I don't shout at him and wake other patients on the floor. "I'm not even a resident yet. I don't have enough credentials. And I do follow that code, to a degree. Your assessment was based on your performance. Your fellow surgeons would have been the ones talking, not me."

Jake stares at me for a moment, then looks at Lauren, who is clearly not amused. She's giving him an evil eye, one so fierce, he isn't able to hold her gaze for very long. He looks down at his feet instead, runs his fingers through his hair, and sighs. A few agonizing seconds later he seems to have collected his thoughts.

"Well, I guess I should stop flirting with the patients... maybe work a little harder... or you'll be chief of surgery before I am."

In this moment, I pity him. I always thought he was the one resident here who'd go far and fast, but that's not the case anymore.

"Get better soon. We need you back in the ER." He nods at me and quickly leaves the room.

## 34. BRAND NEW UNIVERSE

**LAUREN**

Sam licks his spoon, puts it down beside the three empty Jell-O cups, leans back and pats his belly. He looks like he's about to fall asleep, so I kiss his forehead and stand up to leave.

"I'll let you get some rest."

"No, no, Wren, stay if they don't kick you out of here." He takes my hand and pulls me back down beside him.

"Well, there are a few things bothering me..." I say, hesitating to finish my thought.

"Go ahead. I doubt I can sleep in a hospital anyway."

"What? You're going to be a resident soon; you'll have to sleep here!"

"Sleep? Oh sure." He chuckles. "I know Saif will be a wonderful Chief, but he'll put us all to work. You can bet on it." He gently rubs my hand with his thumb. "Okay, go ahead, ask me anything."

"Why do you think Braden went to find Jake?" I ask. "How did he even know Jake worked here?"

"I can tell you why," a female voice answers my question.

Who the bloody hell is it now? Will visiting hours ever be over? I turn my gaze to the door and find Brittany standing there, holding a bouquet of carnations. I despise carnations. They feel like fake flowers, especially the ones that are dyed, and these are hot pink, blue and purple. She looks remorseful, which is surprising, because I didn't know she had that in her.

Brittany saunters up to us and sits on the bottom right corner of Sam's bed, staring at the flowers in her lap as she speaks. "I'm so sorry you got hurt, Lauren, and that Sam got shot. This was supposed to be fun, to help

199

us get popular, and it just blew up so quickly!" Her breathing is uneven, and her face is crimson.

Is she about to ugly cry? Oh God, she's definitely starting to ugly cry, and it looks genuine. Could it be that Brittany actually has some humanity left in her? Well, I won't let my guard down. She and The Laurens made my life here at school unbearable.

"What was supposed to be fun, Brittany? Tell us." I glare at her.

She wrings her hand around the bottom of the bouquet. "Lauren J. told me that she was in touch with that reporter, Braden, from the very start. We had no idea about his mental problems, though. When the buzz started dying down, she told me she had to keep it going, so she emailed Braden photos of you and Jake kissing."

"How the..." I can't even imagine how Lauren managed this.

"She hid in the bushes at the hospital one day. I know, I know. I should have told you how freaky she was getting, but you'd already moved out..." She takes a deep breath in, exhales and looks at me hopefully, as if I'm going to forgive her for her multitude of sins this very minute.

"That's not only sick, that's a bloody invasion of privacy!" I shout.

"She called it clickbait, whatever that means?" She twirls the end of her ponytail with two fingers. "She thought if the story kept going viral, so would her Twitter and Insta accounts. She got really obsessed with her following. It made her a completely different person."

I wonder what kind of person Brittany thought Lauren J. was in the first place and want to ask if she's ever heard of the phrase misery loves company.

"She kept asking me to retweet whatever #laurenfromlastnight tweets she put out. But when that psycho attacked you, I couldn't keep doing it. It just felt... immoral."

My mouth is wide open. I have no words. This girl once let strangers shag in my bed, and now she's talking about morality. Can a person mature in just four months? Then again, I know that I have.

200

"I stopped helping her after that, but she kept texting me her plans. I kept it all, if that helps..." With that confession, Brittany hands Sam the flowers, and he promptly hands them right back to me. I walk to the windowsill and slam them down there.

"What do you mean by *accounts*?" I turn back to her, my hand on one hip.

"She has a few. She made a bunch with the name Lauren and fake last names. She said Braden created bots which automatically retweeted everything she posted. Even while he was locked up, those bots were working for him. I knew it was wrong the minute I heard about it, but I didn't know how to stop Lauren, or him. It just got out of control." She stands and looks at us, awkwardly clasping her hands at her chest as if in prayer.

Hank walks in the room, a grim look on his face, and I rush over to hug him. It's such a relief to see my brother right now. "Hey. I thought you were having pie with everyone?"

"Had to pass. Got caught up talking to some fellows in the RCMP; they're questioning Lexy and other every other witness downstairs. Dad's hired a lawyer. We can press charges against anyone who shared details online about you after your first attack. This Braden creep had a whole army of bots working to keep your story viral. It's clear he was fixated on you, Sam and Jake because of information he got on social media, mostly from a student named Lauren Johnston."

"We know Lauren J. But how did he access a phone if he was in bloody custody?" I ask.

"That, they don't know yet." Hank furrows his brow. "The remaining guard in the psych ward confided in me that the penal system's a mess. He said he has stories that would make you lose sleep at night."

"Hank, after all I've gone through, I'm betting I will be losing sleep at night," I say, not sure if I should laugh or cry at this truth.

He pulls me in for another hug. "Not if I can help it. We'll get you through this. You too, Sam. You're part of the family now, mate."

201

Sam nods and holds out his hand, and Hank leans in and shakes it.

"Thanks for investigating, Hank. With you and Lauren's father working on this, justice will be served," Sam says. He turns to Brittany. "You have to share the story you told us to the police," he says. "If you tell them everything you know, you'll probably get off with lighter charges."

Brittany looks at the floor, scuffing the toe of her boot on the tile, then looks at me.

"Okay. I'm so sorry, Lauren," she says. I give her a blank stare, needing time to digest all of this.

Hank nods at us both. "I'll take her downstairs. See you later." He takes Brittany by the elbow and escorts her out of the room.

"She did sound kind of sorry..." I say, watching her go. "But I hope I never have to hear that bloody awful Barbie voice again."

Sam laughs. "It takes all kinds," he says. "Well, if you're actually ready for jokes, I'd like to add that I feel very lucky that Braden wasn't the serial machete killer I read about last week."

"Serial machete killer?"

"Yeah. Being shot in the stomach is one thing, but being sliced up like sushi by a machete..." He draws in air between his teeth. I laugh and sit beside him on the sliver of space that's left.

"You're something else. You very nearly died, and you're making macabre jokes."

"Well, a wise person once told me that you have to decide if we live in a friendly universe or a hostile universe," he says.

"That wise person was me, right?" Moving my body close to his, I lift my legs off the floor and rest my head on his chest. "It's bloody fucking hostile. I've decided." I laugh because it's the only fighting strength I have left.

"Yup, I agree. The world's gone mad," he says. "But you have a lovely, quiet little apartment, and your landlords make a mean samosa. Once I'm out of here, we can hide away there all winter long, if you want. It will be our little universe." He strokes my hair, then adds, as if reading my thoughts, "Not that I believe it's wise to run away from one's problems. But sometimes, I think it's okay to take a break from everything this wired world demands from us. To unplug and just be."

"That sounds nice, Sam," I say sleepily. "Actually, that sounds perfect."

Heather Grace Stewart

# 35. A CELEBRATION OF MIRACLES

## SAM

"I thank you for coming to Christmas dinner with us, a Christian holiday. It has surprised me." Ma stands, raising her wine glass to everyone at the dining table, which includes my parents, Saif and Farida, Lauren's parents, Lexy, Hank, Béa and their ten-month-old son, Reece.

At the mention of religion, I feel my ears turning six shades of red. Who is this bold woman and where has she been? Not only is she speaking English to a group, but she has invited "those people" into her home with love and an open mind. I never thought I'd see this day.

"Just because we don't celebrate Christmas doesn't mean we can't enjoy a good meal and good company." Saif puts down his water glass and smiles at Ma. "We even put up a Christmas tree this year. Farida finds the lights lovely, so I started doing this for her." He takes his wife's hand, hesitates for a second, then adds, "You know, Muslims believe that Jesus's mother Mary is one of the greatest women to ever live, and a chapter of the Qur'an is devoted to her."

"My goodness! I did not know that!" The three of them lean in and clink glasses. "You must tell us more about your beliefs and customs," Ma says.

I'm so caught off guard with her comment, I nearly fall face first into Farida's Tikki Masala dish. This wouldn't be such a bad thing; her chicken has the most exquisite yogurt marinade I've ever tasted in my life. It would, however, be slightly embarrassing and problematic in front of giggly little Reece who is sitting in his highchair beside me. He seems to worship and copy every movement I make.

As everyone at the table becomes more animated in cheerful conversation, Reece begins clapping his hands, spraying Tikki Masala and rice everywhere. I look over at his mother Béa, and she gives me that terrified parent-as-guest look that says, "Mount your horses! Draw your swords! Fuck if I know! Anything could happen!"

Her eyes are wide, and she's not eating. Hank gives her a reassuring wink and blows out the candles in the silver candelabra that's within Reece's reach. He seems fascinated with the smoke for about half a second. Then, I hear a kitten wailing. Ah. Yes, Lauren brought Snowflake, and now Reece is pulling her tail under the table. As Hank picks Reece up and speaks to him, I get up and move the kitten into the closed-off kitchen where she can lick her wounds in private.

Pouring myself a glass of wine at the buffet, I lean back against the wall to watch everyone laughing and eating at the table. It's lovely to see the people we love getting along and enjoying themselves. I can't believe we fit all these people into this small dining room. Lauren's parents plan to fly back to the UK tomorrow to celebrate Christmas with Lauren's sister and family. Her mother apologized that it took a few emergencies to scare her into this realization: Perhaps they can't be partners, but they'll always be family.

This gathering has been a lot like my days in the ER: one small crisis averted, then it's onto the next one. I'm just grateful to be alive to witness it, and it wouldn't be Christmas without chaos.

I shouldn't be calling it Christmas. Ma called each of our guests to invite them and warned them that this would not be a traditional turkey dinner, but "a multicultural celebration of miracles." That's what she called it. As a result, Farida brought her now-famous Taco Samosa, the Masala and naan bread, and Lauren and I made Vaca Frita, which literally means "fried cow." What can I say, we Cubans like to tell it like it is.

Earlier today, Lauren and I had fun cooking in Farida's kitchen. I marinated the beef in lime, garlic and salt and then Lauren seared it in a pan until it became almost crispy. Ma is also serving shrimps in coconut sauce with steamed rice. Lauren's parents bought delicious pies from the Starry Night café.

There's raucous laugher, so I put my wine at my place and sit down beside Pa and Ma to see what the fuss is all about.

"Here, I think I saw that photo in the buffet cabinet the other day," I hear Ma say to Lauren and Lexy. She gets up from the table, grabs a photo album from the cabinet, and returns.

"Ah yes!" she says, flipping to a page in the middle. She pulls out one photo from behind a plastic sleeve. "Here it is!"

"Aw, how adorable!" Lauren says. "My Superman!" Everyone leans in or gathers around Ma so they can see the photo, and soon there are more "aws" and plenty of laughter.

I'm about eight years old in the photo. I'm hanging from our backyard tree, wearing bright blue tights and a red cape with a big S on it. Sierra's sitting on the branch beside me wearing green scrubs, a fake headlamp and a stethoscope around her neck. I'd completely forgotten about that. We spent the whole day up in that tree.

I'm not a man who believes in signs, and the only person in charge of my destiny is me. Still, I know how fatal gunshots to the abdomen can be. I have to believe Sierra was there with me that day. Saif performed the miracle surgery, but his hands were guided. That's why I agree with Ma: today is a Celebration of Miracles.

I pull up the chair beside my mother and put my arm around her shoulder. I will need to console her over this sudden recollection of Sierra. I hope she doesn't have to leave the room.

When I look at Ma's face, I'm surprised to realize she's not staring at the photo anymore. She's looking around the table at everyone gathered, laughing at something that Lauren just said.

"Can I have this?" I point to the photo.

"Yes, sure. Put it beside that EdgeWalk photograph you have framed in your room." She smiles as she hands me the small square photo. "That day you two skipped school."

207

Mothers. Somehow, they always know.

"Here, take my jacket." I slip off my down, waterproof jacket, brush away snow from our wooden porch swing, and place the jacket down on the seat, motioning for Lauren to sit beside me.

"Well then, you'll just be in a sweater! What about your wound? Won't it get cold?" She keeps standing.

"Wren. I'll be fine." I pat my bandaged abdomen. "I've lived here longer, so I'm used to this cold. Plus..." I pull a plaid blanket from behind my back. "I'm going to be a doctor. Always prepared. Or, truthfully, my Pa is."

As Lauren sits, I wave at Pa and give him the thumbs-up sign he's been waiting for. He's in the window, fervently nodding, making kissing faces and grinning like a chimp in the zoo. *Alright, Pa, alright, a little privacy please.* I give him one more smile and wave him on his way. He moves to the dining buffet, his back turned to us, and hands a drink to Lauren's dad.

"Sam, I could live here another twenty years and never be used to this bloody cold. Brrr!" She pulls the plaid blanket up to our necks, then pushes the ground with her boots, setting us swinging.

It's snowing lightly, but we're covered by the porch roof, which I think is the best way to watch snow fall. The snowflakes are large, fluffy, and because of the porch lights, they're glowing brighter than all the stars in this velvet sky. I see a hint of a smirk on Lauren's face and realize she's enjoying this more than she wants to let on.

"You'd live here twenty years?" I take her hand under the blanket.

"Well, I have a reason to now, don't I?" Lauren looks up at me, her eyes reflecting the pretty white lights hanging from our porch awning. I cup her face with my hand, not caring that my fingers are exposed to the cold night air. She'll keep me warm. Kissing her feels like the first day of every season, like the top of the Ferris wheel and the crest of a crashing wave. Holding her feels like coming home.

# 36. MY LAST DIARY ENTRY

*May 11*

*Dear Diary,*

*I've decided I don't need to keep a diary any longer. Diaries are good therapy, I suppose, but so is talking about my problems with Sam or Lexy or—can you believe it? Mum. She came to stay for spring break. You'd think I'd promptly hyperventilate and pretend I was sick or something, but she's really trying to make amends for her past behavior. We ate at fancy restaurants, we shopped; Sam and I even introduced her to 3D glow in the dark mini golf!*

*Things will never be perfect between us, our broken family never completely patched up. What's perfect, anyway? We do love one another, that part is obvious now. Sometimes we have odd ways of showing it, that's all.*

*Everyone's different; we all show affection differently. Take Brittany. Would you believe she and I have started jogging together? When she texted and asked me, I figured I needed to get out to the lakeside with someone besides Sam. It's not like we're going to be BFFs or anything, but everyone deserves a second chance. Turns out she doesn't like bars or drinking, she was just trying to fit in. She knows all kinds of fitness tips, she's way smarter than I thought, has a big heart, and is actually quite a bit of fun when she's not bloody trying to be the most popular girl on campus. Our new friendship has made me realize I* need to open myself up more, give more people a chance before judging who they are inside.

Because really, we're all the same and different, all at once.

In the end, we're all just snowflakes trying to make our way safely through the storm.

THE END

# GLOSSARY AND REFERENCE

## Lauren and Lexy's Dictionary of London Street Slang – 2020

**allow that:** stop that. Quit doing that. "Allow that right now!"

**bangin':** really good, amazing. "That song was bangin'."

**bare jokes:** very funny. Can also be used in a sarcastic way if it's actually not funny. "Ha! That's bare jokes!"

**chirpsing:** chatting up, flirting with, i.e. "Brittany is chirpsing the bartender."

**ends:** where you come from, where you grew up. "We're from different ends."

**fam:** close family, mates. "You're my fam, always will be."

**mingin':** Ugly, disgusting. "I thought her dress was mingin'."

**to have beef with:** have a problem with; have unresolved issues with someone. "Lexy will have beef with me about this." "Dad and I have unresolved beef."

**Resource:**
**Real London Slang:** Eat Sleep Dream English on Youtube.com

# FARIDA's TACO SAMOSA RECIPE

My mother worked with a woman from Mexico. They became friends, decided to mix these two different recipes from their different cultures. Mother calls it Taco Samosa.

Makes 8 Taco Samosa.

## Taco Shells:

- 1 cup all-purpose flour
- ¼ cup fine sooji (semolina)
- ¼ tsp salt
- ¼ tsp oil
- 3 cup lukewarm water

## The Filling:

- 2 cups potatoes, boiled, peeled and chopped into small cubes
- ½ cup green peas. Frozen green peas is okay.
- 2 tbsp oil (canola or vegetable)
- ½ tsp cumin seeds
- 1 tsp coriander powder
- ¼ tsp red chili powder
- ¼ tsp garam masala
- 1 tsp mango powder (amchur)
- 1 tsp salt
- 2 tbsp green chilies (chop and adjust to taste)
- oil to fry

**For Serving**

- ¼ cup cilantro chutney

- ¼ cup tamarind chutney

**Method :**
**Dough:**

1. Mix the flour and the sooji, salt, oil.

2. Add water as needed to make a firm dough.

3. Knead the dough for about a minute until it is smooth and pliable.

4. Let the dough sit for 15 minutes or more.

**Filling:**

1. Heat the oil in a frying pan on medium heat.

2. Test the heat by adding one cumin seed to the oil. If it cracks right away the oil is ready.

3. Add cumin seeds. As they crack, add green peas. Stir fry for two minutes.

4. Add all other ingredients, potatoes, coriander powder, red chili powder, garam masala, mango powder, salt and green chili. Stir fry for about two minutes. Potato filling should be moist and not dry.

**Making the Taco Shells:**

1.  Knead the dough for a few seconds.

2.  Divide dough into eight equal parts. Then roll each part into a dough ball.

3.  Roll each dough ball into about a 4-inch diameter.

4.  Prick each rolled up Taco with a fork in several places, on both sides, this will prevent Taco from puffing and make them crisp.

5.  Heat the oil in a frying pan over medium heat. The frying pan should have about 1 inch of oil. To check if the oil is ready, put a small piece of dough in the oil. The dough should sizzle and come up slowly.

6.  Place one rolled Taco in the frying pan and press with a skimmer, turn and fold in half. Doing this makes it the taco shape. Do not press! Between the fold there should be space to fill the potatoes filling.

7.  Gently do the next one same way but do not overcrowd the frying pan. Fry them until light golden brown on both sides. This should take about 2-3 minutes.

8.  Take the Tacos out and place them on paper towels to absorb the excess oil. Repeat the process for remaining Tacos.

You can prepare the taco shells in advance and store them in an airtight container.

**Recipe is from Manjula's kitchen. For more recipes like this one,** visit www.manjulaskitchen.com

Heather Grace Stewart

# CARLOS SANCHEZ ON GROWING AND CUTTING ASTERS

**Asters**, daisy-like perennials with star-shaped flower heads, bring such a lovely color to the garden in late summer and autumn when many of your other summer blooms start fading.

The plant is so versatile, you can use it almost anywhere: borders, rock gardens, or wildflower gardens. Asters also attract bees and butterflies, which is good for our planet.

### Choosing and Preparing a Planting Site

- Asters prefer climates with cool, moist summers—especially cool night temperatures. Area 5b where the Sanchez family lives in Edwin Cove is perfect! In warmer climates, plant asters in areas that avoid the hot mid-day sun.

- Select a site with full to partial sun.

- I find that the soil should be moist but well-drained.

- I always mix some compost into the soil prior to planting.

### Starting Seeds Early?

- You can start your seeds indoors during the winter by sowing seeds in pots or flats and keeping them in the refrigerator for 4 to 6 weeks to simulate winter dormancy. Sow seeds one inch deep. After 4 to 6 weeks, put the seeds in a sunny spot in your home. Plant outside after the danger of frost has passed. You can check the last frost dates for your area on the Internet.

- The best time to plant young asters is in mid- to late spring. Fully-grown, potted asters may be planted as soon as they become available in your area.

- I usually space my asters 1 to 3 feet apart, depending on the type and how large they are expected to get.

- Give plants plenty of water at the time of planting.

- I like to add some mulch after planting to keep soil cool and prevent weeds. Sometimes I use bark chips, but I have also used cut grass clippings and that works just fine.

## Care
## How to Grow Asters

- Add a thin layer of compost (or a portion of balanced fertilizer) with a 2-inch layer of mulch around the plants every spring to encourage lots of growth.

- We get lots of rain in Edwin Cove, but if you receive less than 1 inch of rain a week, remember to water your plants regularly during the summer. However, many asters are moisture-sensitive; if your plants have too much moisture or too little moisture, they will often lose their lower foliage or not blossom well. Keep an eye out for any stressed plants and try a different watering method if your plants are losing flowers.

- Stake the tall varieties in order to keep them from falling over.

- Pinch back your asters once or twice in the early summer to promote bushier growth and more blooms. Do not worry about doing this part, they will love you for this!

- Cut back your asters in winter after the foliage has died or leave them through the winter to add some off-season interest to your garden. Aster flowers that are allowed to mature fully may reseed themselves but resulting asters may not bloom true.

- Divide every 2 to 3 years in the spring to maintain your plant's vigor and flower quality.

## Harvest/Storage

Asters work so well as cut flowers! I have learned in my over 40 years as a gardener that there are ways to make flowers stay fresh longer.

## When to Cut Fresh Flowers

- It's important to cut your garden flowers in the morning or early evening when the stalks are filled with water. Midday heat is very stressful to plants. The heat will make them wither.

- Do not pick your flowers when they are in full bloom, or they will not last in your bouquet. Pick them when they are just starting to show color. This is not true of one flower I know though, and that is roses. Roses do not continue to bloom after you cut them, so for that flower, you should wait until you see a medium-sized colourful bloom and then cut your rose.

## How to Cut Flowers

- Always use a sharp knife. Do not use scissors because these can pinch the water channels of the stalks.

- Place the stems straight into a bucket of clean water as soon as you can after cutting.

- If possible, leave the flowers in their bucket of water in a cool, dark spot for a few hours to let them stabilize before you arrange them. Even better, leave them overnight.

- Keep flowers as cool as possible, but don't put them in your fridge, if you can. Florists' coolers range in temperature from 33°to 40°F, so your fridge likely won't be cool enough and any fruits or vegetables could let off ethylene gas, which shortens the life of cut flowers.

Resource: Almanac.com

# About the Author

Heather Grace Stewart is a Canadian author, poet and journalist who writes fast-paced, humorous and touching romance novels. The Ticket, a romantic comedy inspired by a true story, became an International Kindle bestseller and is garnering attention from film and television producers. The Ticket and her first novel Strangely, Incredibly Good were finalists in the Tale Flick Discovery Contest where books are elected to be adapted to the screen.

Heather's second romantic comedy in the Love Again Series, *Good Nights,* was a *TopShelf Magazine* 2019 Books Awards Finalist in humor/comedy. All of her novels are now published audio books with Dreamscape Media and Tantor Audio. She is represented by The Metamorphosis Literary Agency, USA. Please contact agent Stephanie Hansen for all audio, film and foreign rights inquiries.

After receiving her BA (Honours) in Canadian Studies at Queen's University in Kingston, Ontario, Heather attended Montreal's Concordia University for a graduate diploma in Journalism. She worked as chief reporter of a local paper and associate editor of *Harrowsmith Country Life* and *Equinox* magazines before starting her own freelance writing and editing business, Graceful Publications, in 1999.

In her free time, Heather loves to spend time with her husband and daughter, take photos, practice yoga, inline skate, garden, bake bread, dance like nobody's watching, and sample craft beer—usually not at the same time.

Visit her official website at https://heathergracestewart.com/ and sign up for her Readers Club on the front page or at this link https://mailchi.mp/hgrace/join-author-heather-grace-stewarts-readers-club to get a free e-book and to be entered in contests.

Follow her on:

Bookbub: https://www.bookbub.com/authors/heather-grace-stewart

Twitter: @hgracestewart

Instagram: @heathergracestewart

Facebook: https://www.facebook.com/heathergracestewart

Visit Heather's Amazon Author Page: https://www.amazon.com/Heather-Grace-Stewart/e/B007GRA4Y2.

Check out Heather's Audible Books—Also available wherever audio books are sold. Lauren from Last Night Coming August 2020! https://www.audible.com/author/Heather-Grace-Stewart/B007GRA4Y2

## About the Illustrator

Kayla Mae Stewart is a 15-year-old high school student with a passion for art. At five years old she illustrated Heather's book of children's poems, *The Groovy Granny*. Kayla loves cats, science, and her bed.

You can visit her and view more of her artwork on Instagram: @silverleaf_49.

Made in the USA
Middletown, DE
03 September 2021